# GLOOMY GUS

# GLOOMY GUS
## by
## Walt Morey

Blue Heron Publishing, Inc.
Hillsboro, Oregon

# GLOOMY GUS

First Walt Morey Adventure Library edition published 1989
by arrangement with the author.

Cover art copyright © 1988 by Fredrika Spillman

First published by E. P. Dutton & Co., Inc. New York 1976

 Published by
**Blue Heron Publishing, Inc.**
Route 3 Box 376
Hillsboro, Oregon 97124
503/621-3911

ISBN: 0-936085-17-7

Library of Congress Catalog Card Number: 88-072289

Printed in the United States

To trainer Charlie Allen and his Jim bear.

# PART I

❄

# Up North

# - 1 -

ERIC STRONG was sitting with his back against a rock listening to the summer rhythm of the north when he heard the odd, whimpering murmur that did not belong out here on the tundra. He closed his ears to all other sounds and centered his attention on a patch of alders a short way off.

He rose, and with eyes fastened on the spot, tiptoed noiselessly forward and peered into the brush. He looked into the great, furry face of a Kodiak bear. His heart gave a thunderous leap. But, even as panic roared through him, he saw a round hole between the eyes and the trickle of dried blood which snaked across the broad nose. The bear was dead.

Then he saw the source of the soft sounds. A small cub was nuzzling at the dead bear's side, whimpering and pushing as it searched for a spot to nurse. Eric stepped through the brush and squatted near the cub. The cub continued to push at its mother's solid side.

Eric touched the great bear's shoulder. It was cold, and the muscles felt stiff. She had been dead a long time, probably since yesterday, or even the day before. "Gee," he said to the cub, "you're hungry. You must be starving."

The cub turned its head and looked at Eric with small, beady eyes. The next moment it scrambled forward, wrapped its front paws around Eric's arm, and climbed up against his chest. It began sucking on a button of his old sweater, making the soft, nursing sounds.

Eric put his arms around the small body and felt it trem-

3

bling. It kept sucking on the button. Eric stroked the soft fur and said, "You're awful cold, and you sure are hungry. I've got to get you warm and find you something to eat, or you'll die." He looked around helplessly at the towering snow-capped peaks ringing the horizon, as though he might find these needs nearby. It was too early in the summer for berries. The salmon weren't yet running in the spawning streams, and the cub was too young to eat fish anyway. It couldn't eat roots, herbs, and grass yet.

"You need milk," the boy said. "Bear's milk."

Maybe canned milk would do. Every morning Eric had canned milk diluted with water. But that meant he'd have to take the cub home. He hesitated. His father had not come home last night, but he should be returning about now. From past experiences Eric knew his father would be half sick, and in an ugly mood. At such times he could be cruel. He did not like animals — bears in particular. There was no telling what his father might do to this helpless cub. Maybe if he hurried home he could feed the cub and get it out of the house before his father came. Eric didn't know what he'd do with the cub after he'd fed it, but right now it needed food more than anything.

The cub was apparently exhausted. It slept peacefully in Eric's arms most of the way home. When it awoke for a few minutes, it began sucking on the button again. "That's all right," Eric soothed. "We'll be home soon and then I'll feed you all you can drink."

Eric's home was a two-room, weather-beaten cabin. Of more than a hundred cabins scattered about the outskirts of Tatouche, theirs was the only one still lived in. The rest were in various stages of decay; roofs fallen in, windows broken, doors ripped away, and porches falling down. Theirs was getting that way, but Eric's father didn't worry. It had cost him nothing. When they had come to Tatouche years ago, he'd found it vacant, so he moved in. No one objected. The owners had long been gone.

The story of Tatouche was well known to Eric. It was an

old copper-mining town that squatted on the bank of Tatouche Bay. At the height of its prosperity it had boasted twelve hundred people, a business street four blocks long, and the finest ore dock in all the north. In some eighteen years, more than a hundred million dollars' worth of copper ore had been taken from the hills. A special railroad from the mine had transported the copper to the Tatouche dock. There great ships stopped every week and loaded the rich ore into their holds. Tatouche had been a bustling town. A thousand miners, railroad men, sailors, laborers, and gamblers tramped the wooden sidewalks. There were more than a dozen saloons along Main Street.

Eric often peeked through the boarded-up windows of the biggest saloon, the Copper Lady. It was here, people said, that men gambled and drank on weekdays, then worshipped on Sunday before an altar let down from the ceiling by ropes. They had placed their contributions in beer mugs.

Then the rich copper vein ran out and the mine closed down. The railroad tracks leading ten miles into the hills to the mine were rusted, the crossties rotting. The mine was deserted, the tunnels were caving in and overgrown with weeds. Gradually the people drifted away from Tatouche. Now less than a hundred remained. The business district had shrunk to a scant block. Only one of the bars, Eddie Lang's, was still open. It did little business. The town was kept barely alive by prospectors and trappers and a few seine boats which headquartered here during the fishing season.

The inhabitants still talked about the town's great past and never ceased to hope it would revive. Ever since he could remember, Eric had heard the predictions. "Someone will uncover a new rich vein of copper. Where there's been so much, there must be more. Maybe one of the big fish companies will put in a cannery. Some big outfit will surely build a sawmill. These mountains are full of good timber. Someday great ships will be tied to the dock again and Tatouche will boom once more." But twenty years had passed and no ship had entered the bay to tie up at the dock.

Eric approached the cabin warily, holding the whimpering cub close in his arms. If his father was home, the door would probably be open this warm, sunny morning. Just possibly there'd be a fire in the stove.

The door was closed, and no smoke issued from the rusty stovepipe. He opened the door carefully and went inside.

The cabin was small. It had one fairly large room with his father's bunk nailed to one wall. Across the room was an old four-burner wood stove with three plank shelves above it. They held a thin assortment of canned food, cereals, and several loaves of bread. A rough, homemade table with three rickety chairs sat in the middle of the room. A couple of rifles and a shotgun leaned in a corner. A wolverine pelt and two wolf hides hung on the wall. In back was a smaller room, just big enough for Eric's cot and the few articles of clothing similar to the old sweater and patched overalls he was wearing.

Eric put the cub on his father's bed. It snuggled down among the old covers and began sucking on a piece of cloth. "You wait," Eric said. "I'll get you something to eat right away."

He found half a can of condensed milk and emptied it into a pan. He added an equal amount of water and stirred it with his finger.

He took the cub from the bed, sat on the floor, held it between his legs, and began to feed it. He spooned up milk, then tried to force the cub's mouth open to insert the spoon. The cub whimpered and tossed his head, spilling the milk. Eric filled the spoon and tried again. "Open your mouth," he coaxed. "This is what you've been wanting. You have to eat or you're going to starve. This is good." He held the spoon against the cub's lips hoping he'd get a taste of milk and open his mouth. The cub whimpered, shook his head, and spilled the milk again. Eric spooned up more milk. "Now, look," he said, "I'm only trying to help you. Can't you understand that? This is milk. Taste it. Smell it. Bears are supposed to have good noses. Don't be so stubborn. Open your mouth and taste it, then you'll know. Open up, you hear..." He was so busy trying to get the cub to drink he didn't hear the door open. When he looked up, his father was standing there, scowling.

Eric's father was not old, as Eric thought of old men. But he looked old with his red-blotched face, bloodshot eyes, and sagging checks. He was short with a round, heavy body and a bullet-shaped head covered with straight black hair. He swayed slightly on thick legs, looking down at the boy and the cub.

"I found him out on the tundra," Eric explained quickly holding the squirming cub to him. "Somebody killed his mother. He's awfully hungry, Pa. He's starving."

"A bear cub. A Kodiak cub!" His father's voice was thick. "You know better'n to bring a thing like that in this house. It's bad enough they run loose on the tundra, eatin' fish and things. Get 'im outa here — now! Go on, get 'im out."

"Pa, he's starving. I couldn't leave him to die."

"Better he starves now," his father said. "If he grows up, somebody'll just have to shoot 'im. It's too expensive to feed a dumb bear. It takes most all I earn to feed you. Only good bear's a dead one."

"He won't eat much," Eric begged. "He's just a baby, Pa. He can't feed himself yet or anything. He needs somebody to care for him and look out for him, till he grows a little more. He can have part of my milk."

"If you don't drink milk, you'll eat something else," his father grumbled. "It adds up."

"But not for long, Pa. As soon as he gets big enough to look out for himself, I'll turn him loose."

"No, you won't. I know you, kid. You'll wanta keep 'im, and that bear'll wanta stay." His father leveled a finger at Eric. "No animals! You know that. Especially no bears. Now you get that thing outa here, and no more arguments. You understand that, kid?"

Eric wished his father would call him anything but "kid." "Please, Pa," he begged, "just this once. Just for a little while, till he's big enough to look out for himself. I'll turn him loose, I promise. I've never had anything, Pa. Never…"

The cub was squirming in the boy's arms, and suddenly he broke loose and went scrambling across the floor toward the man's legs murmuring "Mmmmm-mmmm-mmm."

Ned Strong drew back a heavy foot and slammed it into the cub's stomach. The cub wailed in surprise and pain. The kick lifted him cartwheeling out the open door, where he fell sprawling in the weed-infested yard.

Eric started up, crying, "You hurt him, Pa! You hurt him!"

His father slammed the door. "Leave 'im be," he snapped. "You ever bring that animal in the house again I'll kill 'im." He walked unsteadily to the bed and sat down heavily. "We got any coffee?"

"The pot's half full."

"Get a fire goin' and heat it up."

"I'll get some wood."

"There's wood in the box." His father leaned forward, bloodshot eyes fixed on the boy. "You don't fool me, kid. Don't ever let me catch you messin' around with that Kodiak cub again. Now get that fire goin'."

Eric stuffed paper in the firebox, added a handful of kindling, and lit it. He removed one of the lids and put the coffeepot over the open hole. He kept thinking about the cub. His father had kicked him awfully hard. The bear had struck the ground with a solid thump. He was very young and small to withstand such punishment. Eric listened, hoping to hear the whimpering, murmuring sounds. But the crackling fire drowned out any other noises.

Soon the coffee was hot. Eric filled a cup and took it to his father. He had fallen flat on his back on the bed, legs dangling over the side of the bunk. He was sound asleep. Probably he'd not wake for hours.

Eric and his father were different in many ways. Eric's bones were long, even for an eleven-year old. He would never have that blocky, thick build. His features were fine, his hair was almost blond. There was a gentleness in his smile and

8

gray eyes that his father did not have. His father had said he took after his mother. But he'd never talk about her.

"She's long dead," he had said when Eric had asked about her. "Does no good talkin'. Got rid of everything, even pictures. It's best to forget."

But Eric could not help thinking about his mother. He pictured her tall, slender, with blonde hair and laughing eyes. Her voice was gentle. The touch of her hands was as soft as the caress of a leaf. She'd listen to a boy with understanding and love. He wondered what she had ever seen in his father.

Eric pulled his father farther up onto the bed and spread a blanket over him. He poured the coffee back into the pot and moved it off the fire. Then he tiptoed out the door and closed it softly after him.

The cub was huddled against the side of the cabin wall, whimpering. He lifted it gently and probed carefully for broken bones. There seemed to be none. "You're lucky," he murmured, stroking the cub. The cub snuggled down in his arms and began to suck on the button again. "What am I going to do with you?" Eric said. "Pa won't let me keep you. If I take you in the house again, he'll kill you, sure, when he wakes up."

The boy tried to think of someone he could take the cub to. His father's only friends were two old cronies with whom he spent most of his time in the bar. They hated bears. He couldn't take the cub to Mrs. Allen. She already had two cats and a dog.

Eric had no school friends. His father's temper had long ago run off any friends he might have had. In all this town there must be somebody who would take a starving cub.

Then he remembered Ten-Day Watson.

Eric had seen Ten-Day Watson at rare intervals when he came to town for supplies. He was a rugged old man with a great white beard, a broad chest, and heavy shoulders. Scraggly white hair peeked beneath his battered felt hat. His sturdy legs swung him along at an easy stride.

Mostly Eric remembered the old man's eyes. They were

a startling deep-water blue.

He had heard that Watson once raised a wolf cub and a moose calf together. People said there were always some kinds of animals around his cabin.

Eric had never been to Watson's, but he knew the way. He'd have to go through town and out the old gravel road that went to the abandoned airport. Watson's cabin was off the road several hundred yards, on the bank of Friday Creek, about two miles out of town.

Eric held the cub close and hoped no one would see him as he hiked through the town's short street. His father's two cronies were still in Eddie Lang's bar. He hesitated in front of George Summers' grocery store, his eyes drawn to a display in the window of four wristwatches on a cardboard shield. Three were silver, marked $9.98. The fourth was gold and was priced $14.98. He had been admiring the gold one for weeks as he came and went to school, wishing it were his. George Summers came toward the front of the store and Eric went hurriedly on.

He was passing the end of the ore dock when he met Joe Lucky returning empty-handed from where he'd been fishing on the bay end of the dock.

Joe Lucky was tall and unusually thin. He had a shrill, squeaky voice that always sounded excited. During the town's boom days Lucky had operated the only taxicab service in Tatouche. He still ran the old Model A Ford up and down the street and out to the airport a couple of times a month just to keep it in running order. As near as Eric could tell, Joe Lucky seemed to spend most of his time fishing off the end of the dock.

Joe Lucky called, "Hey, Eric, what you got there?"

Eric hurried on, pretending not to hear. Lucky caught his arm and pulled him around. "Well, how about that?" he piped. "A Kodiak Cub. Where'd you get him?"

"I found him," Eric tried to pull away.

"No foolin'. Kind of a cute little bugger, ain't he? Tell you what — let's have some fun. I got a little old dog about his size. Let's turn him and Beans loose together and have us a fight. Ought to be right entertainin'."

"No!" Eric twisted loose and ran.

Joe Lucky's shrill voice called after him, "Don't let that Crazy Watson see him. He'll run him through the sluice boxes, sure."

Eric thought about Ten-Day Watson again as he trudged up the gravel road with the cub cradled in his arms. Crazy, that was what people called him to his back. He had a claim on the creek in front of his cabin. He worked it about two weeks every summer. In that time he took out enough gold to last him the year. For the next eleven and a half months he hiked about the country with a pack on his back, followed by a dog or two. He went no place special, looked at nothing in particular. He was just enjoying living in the fabulous north.

"Crazier than a loon," people said. "Gone up here," and they tapped their heads. "Why don't he work the claim harder when it's so rich? He hates people. He'd rather live with animals — that moose and the wolf he'd raised and turned loose again. He could have killed the moose for his winter's meat and the wolf for the bounty. He's been living alone so many years he got cabin fever and it never left. Crazy, all right."

Eric's steps slowed. How did a crazy man act? What might he do to this helpless cub, or to Eric himself? Maybe it would be better to hide it in one of the empty houses and sneak milk to it. But the cub would be cold and lonesome at night. It might crawl out, get loose, and starve to death. Or someone might find it and kill it.

The cub kept sucking on his sweater button and whimpering.

"There's no place else," Eric said. "I've got to take you up to Ten-Day Watson's. He did raise a wolf cub and that moose calf. And they say he's had other animals. So I guess he's not crazy with animals."

The boy came to a dim trail and turned into it. He was almost there. Just around that short bend ahead was Friday Creek and Crazy Ten-Day Watson's cabin.

# - 2 -

TEN-DAY WATSON'S cabin sat within a few feet of the bank of swift-running Friday Creek. Eric saw the old man several hundred feet up the creek. He had his sluice boxes in the stream and was standing almost knee-deep in the water, industriously shoveling gravel into the boxes. A small deer stood on the bank. Eric watched the man for a minute and decided that shoveling gravel into a sluice box wasn't the act of a crazy man. He walked slowly upstream and stopped on the bank. The deer looked at him with great liquid eyes, flapped its huge ears, and stomped tiny feet. But it didn't offer to run.

Eric watched the man anxiously. He didn't know how to announce his presence and he was at a loss for what to say. Finally Watson looked up. He studied Eric a moment, then waded ashore, stuck the shovel upright in the dirt, and came to stand over him.

Eric backed off a step, clutching the cub tightly. Crazy Ten-Day Watson looked bigger than he had in the water. He was taller than Eric's father, broader and thicker. But his eyes were clear and direct and the flesh of his cheeks was brown and firm.

Watson glowered down at Eric from beneath bushy white brows, big fists on hips, "You shouldn't have took that cub from his mama, boy," Watson said.

"I didn't. I found him on the tundra a couple of miles from town. Somebody had killed his mother. He was trying to nurse. He's awfully hungry. He hasn't had anything to eat for a long time. He's starving."

"Who sent you up here?"

"I just came."

"You figured Crazy Watson would take 'im?"

Eric just stood there.

"Well, I won't," Watson said. "Take him back home. Let your folks keep him."

"Pa kicked him out," Eric said. "He hates bears."

"Give him to your ma. Women are soft that way."

"There's just me and Pa," Eric said.

"Then give him to a friend. You got friends?"

Eric shook his head, "No."

Watson scratched his beard with angry fingers. "Give him to somebody else. Town's full of people."

"Nobody wants a bear," Eric said. "Nobody."

"That's your problem," Watson said exasperated. "Don't come botherin' me with it. I got other things to do besides takin' in every stray that comes along. I got a deer and a pup in the cabin now. That's enough. Take your troubles someplace else."

"Where can I take him?"

"How would I know?"

"He'll die," Eric said. "I don't want him to die."

"Talk to the fool that shot his mother," Ten-Day Watson said. "Go on! Get a move on, boy."

Eric turned and left. The cub kept sucking on the button of his sweater. It was going to die now and there was nothing he could do about it. He had almost reached the trail at the corner of the cabin when Watson called, "Boy! Just a minute."

Watson strode up to him, scowling, scratching his beard with an angry gesture. "All right?" he grumbled. "Can't see anything starve. But mind, I'm doing this for the cub, not for you."

"I know." Eric followed Watson into the cabin. The deer pattered behind Eric, his small hoofs making quick hammer sounds on the plank floor.

The cabin was neat and clean. The walls were lined with shelves, well stocked with food, magazines, books, a hand-crank phonograph, and a stack of records. There were pictures on the walls. A pair of shiny well-oiled rifles leaned in a corner beside a stack of shallow iron containers used for panning gold. Watson's made-up bed was in another corner. A Yukon stove stood near one wall with a table and four chairs nearby. A huge Kodiak rug covered the center of the floor. A malamute pup, about the size of the cub, crawled from under the stove. He was blinking his eyes and yawning sleepily.

Watson patted the pup and asked, "You have a good snooze, Kenai?"

The pup wagged his tail.

Watson dug through a drawer in the table and found an old leather glove.

"I tried to feed him milk with a spoon, but he wouldn't drink," Eric said.

"He's too young to drink. He needs to nurse." Watson punched a hole in a can of condensed milk and emptied it into a pan. He added water and stirred it. Then he poured the glove full. He puckered the top and punched a pinhole in the end of the glove's biggest finger. "All right," he said, "sit on the floor and hold the cub in your lap."

They sat on the bear rug facing each other, and Ten-Day Watson shoved the punched finger against the cub's lips. The cub got the idea immediately. It grabbed the forefinger and began to suck, murmuring "Mmmm — mmmm-mmmm." It wrapped both forepaws around Watson's big hand and closed its eyes in ecstasy.

Kenai and Sitka, the deer, came to investigate. Sitka flapped his big ears, stomped his tiny hoofs, and snorted delicately at the bear smell. The pup waved his tail and stuck his nose up. Watson shoved them away. "Beat it, you've both been fed."

Kenai went off a few feet, sat on his tail, ran out his tongue and grinned. Sitka backed out of reach and watched, big eyes fastened on the cub.

The cub emptied the glove without stopping. Watson filled it again and the cub emptied it a second time. Eric could feel his stomach getting round and hard. The cub was suddenly full and squirmed out of Eric's arms. He spotted Kenai and scrambled clumsily across the rug to the dog. They touched noses. Kenai's tail waved happily and he licked the cub's black nose. The cub stood on hind legs and placed both front paws around the pup's neck. The next moment they were tumbling across the floor, wrestling and growling in play. Sitka stamped his feet, prepared for flight.

The old man and the boy sat on the rug and watched. Eric saw the sternness leave the old man's face as he began to smile.

The wrestling went on for several minutes. Small bodies rolled about on the chair legs, the table, the stove. First one, then the other, was on top. They ended up on the bear rug, nose to nose, panting, glaring, and growling. The cub now wanted a nap. He curled up on the rug, front paws under his chin. Kenai lay down beside him. In a minute they were asleep, their small heads close together.

Sitka shook his head disdainfully and trotted out the door.

"What're you going to do with your cub?" Watson asked. "He'll die if you turn him loose."

"*My* cub?" Eric asked, surprised.

"You found him. You saved him from dyin'."

Eric looked at the small cub sleeping peacefully beside Kenai. A great warmth surged through him. For the first time in his life he owned something. But the feeling was almost immediately gone. "I can't keep him," he said miserably, "and nobody wants a bear."

Watson rose and stood looking at the cub, big hands shoved into his pockets. "Bear cubs can be the gloomiest-looking little beggars," he said thoughtfully, "and he's about the gloomiest Gus I ever saw."

"What's that?" Eric asked.

"Gloomy Gus? Just a saying. It means someone that's got more troubles than he can handle. And a cub that's lost his mama and is starving has got all the troubles there is." He scratched his beard, frowning, annoyed. "I don't want 'im. I've got enough with Sitka and Kenai. But I can't see a cub or a fawnthing starve."

Eric's worry was over. The cub would live. He felt a rush of friendliness for the grumpy, old man. He followed Watson outside and asked, "How long will you have to feed him milk?"

"He'll start eating fish and other things in a couple of months, if it's cut up for him. But he'll need some milk until it's time for him to den up this winter."

"How much milk will he drink a day?"

"Couple of cans."

That would be about forty cents a day, Eric thought. He'd never had forty cents to call his own in his whole life. He said, "I can help some with the mining. I can shovel."

"Why?"

"I should pay for what he eats. I haven't any money."

"Don't need help," Watson started to walk away.

"I'd like to help," Eric said. "I'm strong for eleven."

"Don't want help. Go home, boy." He walked up the bank, got his shovel, waded into the creek again, and began filling the sluice boxes.

Eric watched for a minute, but the old man ignored him. A second shovel leaned against the side of the cabin. Eric took it and waded into the creek on the opposite side of the sluice boxes. He began shoveling gravel into the boxes.

Watson said angrily, "What do you think you're doing?"

"The cub's mine, but you have to keep him and feed him," Eric said in a rush. "That's not right. I have to help somehow."

The boy and the old man looked into each other's eyes across the sluice boxes. Then Watson waded ashore, went to the cabin, and returned with a pair of boots. "They're too big, but they'll keep your feet dry," he grumbled.

For almost an hour they stood on opposite sides of the sluice boxes and worked; neither spoke. Kenai and the cub awoke from their naps and came from the cabin. The pup headed for Watson and the cub followed. They struggled through the long grass to the creek bank and sat down to watch. Sitka quit nibbling leaves from a bush long enough to smell of them. Then he shook his head, snorted delicately, and went back to the bush.

16

The cold of the stream came through the boots and numbed Eric's feet. His arms and shoulders began to ache. Pain crept into the small of his back. He realized Watson was doing this to show him how hard it was, and in that way drive him off. He gritted his teeth, determined to stick it out. Finally Watson said, "We'll knock off awhile," and waded ashore.

Eric followed and sat down tiredly beside the cub. The cub immediately crawled into his lap. Its stomach was still hard and full. It snuggled down and almost immediately went to sleep again. Eric stroked it, smiling.

Watson asked, "What's your name, boy?" Eric told him, and the old man said grudgingly, "You work pretty good for eleven. Your pa gonna be wondering where you are?"

"No," Eric said. "Pa don't ask much where I go or what I do. He's on a seine boat all summer anyway."

"How do you eat?"

"I get my own breakfast and lunch. I have a hot supper with Mrs. Allen every night. She kind of looks after me some. Pa pays her at the end of the fishing season."

"You're alone all summer while your pa seines?"

"Except for weekends when they're not allowed to fish."

"What do you do with your time?"

Eric shrugged. The summers were long and lonesome when you had no friends. "I mostly just wander around," he said. "I can come up and help every day."

"Don't want you up here," Watson said bluntly. "Don't want anybody up here."

Eric remembered what he'd heard people say about the old man, and when his next words popped out, they startled him. "Why don't you like people, Mr. Watson?"

The old man's blue eyes were as cold as the creek water. He said, "It's been a long time since anybody asked me that. But I'll tell you, boy, I was here before they found that copper vein. Deer, moose, fox, bear, all kinds of game animals and birds used to come right down to the cabin. Why, geese and ducks used to nest where we're sittin'. Then they punched holes in the mountains, put in a railroad, and the people poured in. The ore

17

cars and railroad engines clattered and banged all day and night. Smoke and dust filled the air. It seemed like everybody in town had a gun and I never heard so much shootin' in all my life. I found dead animals and birds all over the tundra, like you found that mother Kodiak today. There wasn't hardly a squirrel or a bird for ten miles around Tatouche. Finally the mine shut down and the people left. After a few years the game started coming back. Now the country's fit to live in again. That's the way I want it kept."

Eric stroked the sleeping cub and said, "I wouldn't kill them. I like to watch them. That's how I found the cub. I was watching a fox on that bald hill south of town. She's get a den in the ground and I counted two pups. I think she's got another but he hasn't come out yet. This is the second year she's had pups in the same den. And there's a cow moose down by the lake with a new calf. A mother duck with a bunch of babies was swimming right around the moose's head the other day while she was feeding. They weren't a bit afraid of her."

"Hm-m." Watson studied the boy thoughtfully. Then he rose. "Guess we'd better shovel a little more — if you feel up to it."

The summer was like no other for Eric. His was the responsibility of caring for the cub and earning its food by working for Ten-Day Watson. His days were full and exciting. He bolted his breakfast, then hurried through town before anyone was stirring.

Watson asked once, as they sat on the creek bank resting and Eric played with Gus, "Are you sure your pa don't mind you being up here every day?"

"He doesn't know." Eric scratched the cub's stomach, smiling as Gus stretched luxuriously. "I didn't tell him."

"Don't he ask what you do with your time when he comes home?"

"Sometimes, but he forgets right away. Mostly he just asks Mrs. Allen if everything's all right. She always says 'yes' and he's satisfied. She knows I come up here but she doesn't care.

It's someplace for me to go."

"How come you don't have any kid friends?'

"There's only fourteen kids in school, eight girls and six boys. The girls all play among themselves. I'm older than most of the boys and they sort of stick together because their folks are all friends. Pa doesn't have any friends among them. His friends are just those two old guys he hangs out in the bar with. A couple of times kids did come around, but Pa was mean and drove them away."

"It must be pretty lonesome alone."

"It was till this summer," Eric smiled.

"Guess your pa makes it up to you when he's home all winter."

Eric shook his head. "He traps some to keep us in grub."

"Don't he make enough seining to see you through the winter?"

"No." Eric continued petting Gus and added thoughtfully, "He spends lots of time in Eddie Lang's bar."

"In winter?"

"He says he gets cabin fever sitting around the house all the time."

"Seems like he ought to take more interest in his own flesh and blood," Watson said.

"You mean me?" Eric asked.

"I mean you. A father ought to look out for his son."

Eric rubbed Gus's stomach, his gray eyes dark and thoughtful. "I guess Pa wishes I wasn't around. He's said lots of times if it wasn't for me he wouldn't have to work so hard."

"Looks to me like you pretty much take care of yourself winter and summer."

Eric nodded. Gus rolled off his lap and headed for Kenai, who was napping nearby. "Mrs. Allen helps me out some. She shows me how to cook and do things." He smiled and stretched out a leg and pointed to a new round patch on his knee. "She showed me how to do that."

"Your pa better get you some new ones," Watson observed. "You've about got patches on patches there."

"He likely will when school starts."

Watson shook his head and rose muttering, "Don't understand the man. Just don't understand him."

Eric's father returned on weekends during the fishing season, and he asked once, "What did you do with that Kodiak cub, kid?"

"I gave him to Ten-Day Watson."

"Joe Lucky said he sees you headin' up that way every mornin' and Mrs. Allen says you're gone all day. What're you doin' up there?"

Eric hesitated. He didn't dare tell his father the cub was his and he was helping pay for its food. "Mr. Watson has to buy milk for the cub and I work for him a little to help pay for it," he said lamely.

"Why?" his father demanded.

"I took the cub up to him," Eric explained. "I sort of feel responsible."

"There's no call for you to go up there and help that old coot," his father said.

"I've got nothing else to do all summer. It gets awful lonesome, Pa."

His father grunted and reached for his hat. "You keep hangin' around that old man they'll start callin' you crazy, too," he warned and left.

Eric enjoyed every minute with Ten-Day Watson, Kenai, Sitka, and Gloomy Gus. Gus was a lively, healthy cub. He and Kenai spent hours wrestling in the grass while Eric and Watson worked in the creek. When Eric flopped on the bank to rest, the cub would climb into his lap searching for the soft-drink bottle which had replaced the glove to hold his milk. Eric would scratch at the base of his stubby ears and smile when the cub made contented rumblings in his chest.

All too soon the day arrived when they took the sluice boxes from the creek and piled them against the cabin. Ten-Day Watson was through mining for the year. Eric realized, with a sick feeling, he would not be dashing up here every morning. He said, "You won't need me after today."

"How so?"

"There's nothing more to do," Eric said miserably.

"Oh, that," Watson smiled, his blue eyes squinting at the boy. "We'll find something. See you tomorrow."

In succeeding days they left the animals at the cabin and hiked across the soft, spongy tundra. They followed streams to their sources at the feet of ancient glaciers, then climbed to the surface and walked about. They prospected along lonely beaches and around dozens of jewel-like bays nestling at the feet of mountains or all but hidden by dense stands of virgin timber.

They stopped once to rest in a tiny meadow snuggled into the hollow between the mountains. Eric flopped on his back and stared up into the endless blue sky. A half-dozen peaks encircled them, their tops glistening in the summer sunlight. There was not a whisper of sound. A crow sailed into Eric's vision and out again. A cool breeze funneled down off the high peaks laced with the bite of snowfields. The smell of the earth rose warm and heavy from beneath his head. A rabbit hopped into the open, sat up and studied them a moment, then disappeared. A short way off a crystal stream fled noiselessly toward the sea. Eric turned on his side and studied the water.

When he spoke, his voice was unconsciously hushed. "No spawning salmon. No nothing."

"That's runoff from a glacier," Watson said "It's so pure nothing lives in it."

Eric sat up and hugged his knees. The silence pressed in on him as real as the heat of the day. "It's so quiet, like we're the first people that ever saw this place. I've never been so far from town."

"How long ago did you come here?" Watson asked.

"I don't know. Mrs. Allen says I was about three."

"Your ma come with you?"

Eric shook his head. "She was dead then. I don't remember her."

"You got any uncles or aunts or cousins? Most everybody's got some kind of relatives."

21

"I don't know," Eric said. "I asked Pa a couple of times, but he always gets mad and starts yelling at me. I don't ask anymore."

"Your pa was always a fisherman?"

"No, we came from inland. I think the Kantishna. Pa had some kind of mine. I guess it was no good or something. He won't ever talk about it."

"Funny he's come here, to a town that had died and a mine that had been shut down for years," Watson observed.

"I heard Pa say that he thought these mountains must be full of ore and he figured to make another strike."

"A lot of prospectors thought that way, but they changed their minds and left."

"Pa prospected for a couple of years. Then he got to seining in the summer and never went back to it again."

"Mighty odd," Watson said thoughtfully. "Once a prospector, always a prospector. Wonder how he got it outa his blood so complete?"

Gus grew amazingly. Soon Eric could no longer hold him in his arms. He began eating small chunks of salmon that Eric cut up. The boy held each piece in his palm, smiling as Gus lifted it deftly with just the touch of his soft lips. By fall the bear had outgrown Kenai and Sitka together.

"He'll go two hundred pounds," Watson estimated. "He's going to be a bruiser."

Fishing season ended and Eric went back to school. Frost cut the leaves from the alder and willow thickets. The feathered migrators headed back over the long miles south. The snow line crept down the slopes to the low tundra and waited the first blast of winter to turn the world white.

Gus went to sleep in a hole under Ten-Day Watson's cabin.

# - 3 -

THE SNOW LINE crept back up the slopes into the high hills. The green and yellow tundra lay shining bright and carpet-smooth under the early summer sun. The feathered migrators returned and were nesting all across the tundra. The last of the ice was gone from Friday Creek and the current ran cold and strong.

Eric and Ten-Day Watson were putting the sluice boxes into the creek for the third season. Kenai and Sitka stood on the bank watching. Sitka was full grown with a fine rack of horns. Kenai weighed seventy pounds and showed the part-wolf strain in his black masked face, yellow eyes, and slinking walk.

As they worked, Eric's gaze often strayed out across the fresh tundra toward the distant snow-covered mountains where Gus had disappeared last fall. Finally he said in a worried voice, "It's time for Gus to come back, don't you think Ten-Day?"

"Any day now," Watson agreed. "Fact is, he's probably been out a few days already?"

"Then why doesn't he come?"

"The first couple of days bears just wander around. Their stomachs don't want food yet. Then when they start eating it's green stuff, like new skunk-cabbage shoots, tender green grasses, and roots. He'll spend a couple of days on that. My guess is that he won't come down here until he's had his fill of green stuff."

23

"Do you think he'll remember me?" Eric asked for the hundredth time. "Do bears have good memories, Ten-Day?"

"He'll remember. Why shouldn't he?"

"He was holed up about six months last year and the year before," Watson reminded him.

"It's different this time. He went out in the mountains this winter. The other two he holed up under your cabin. He might have gone fifteen or twenty miles back into those mountains. Maybe that'll make him forget."

"He'll remember. You'll see."

"Where do you suppose he spent the winter?" Eric mused.

"No telling. Maybe in a cave, or he might have dug a hole in the side of a hill, maybe under a fallen tree or an uprooted stump. Whatever place struck his fancy as being a cozy spot. Grab the other end of this box and we'll set it in the creek."

They set the sluice box and waded ashore.

"You've grown about as fast as Gus," Watson observed. He felt Eric's arm. "A little thin yet, but there's muscle there."

Eric smiled, "I'm an inch taller than Pa now. I graduated from school this spring, you know."

Watson nodded. "What do you figure to do now?"

"Work with you this summer the same as before. There's nothing to do in Tatouche. Maybe next year I'll be big and heavy enough so that somebody will take me on a seiner."

"I've been thinking about something," Watson said. "Been meaning to talk to you about it. Gus is on his own now. I don't give him milk or anything. So you can't work here for nothing to help feed him anymore. You've got to be paid for it if you're going to work every day."

"I've got nothing else to do. I like coming up here."

"I like having you," Watson said. "You and me, Kenai and Sitka and Gloomy Gus hit it off fine. But it's not right a boy your size working every day for nothing. You've got to go on the payroll."

"I know you don't have to feed Gus anymore," Eric said.

"But you're always giving him things, like those extra pancakes in the morning and sugar cubes and sugar water."

"The pancakes are leftovers, and sugar cubes and what little goes in the water don't cost much."

"It costs," Eric insisted. "And you bake those extra pancakes on purpose. I know. Maybe you've forgot I eat lunch with you every day. And sometimes supper, too, now that Mrs. Allen don't look out for me anymore."

Watson shook his white head. "A boy your size has got to have a little money to rattle in his pocket. How about five dollars a week?"

"But that'll come out of your winter stake."

"With you helping I take out a lot more dust than I would alone. It comes outa that extra."

"All right," Eric agreed. "Then I'll take it."

That night on the way home he stopped and looked through the window of George Summer's store at the gold watch. The five dollars wouldn't be all clear. He'd have to buy sugar cubes for Gus now and once in a while a shirt or jeans for himself. But in a few weeks he could save enough to buy the watch.

The next morning they'd been working in the creek about an hour when Kenai began barking excitedly. Eric glanced up and there was Gus plodding majestically across the tundra toward them. He was not idling along stopping often to paw and sniff at grass clumps as he had done in the past. He came on steadily, the sun striking golden highlights from his thick brown coat. He moved with lofty assurance, massive head swinging, the great muscles rolling and bunching beneath his loose-fitting hide.

Sitka trotted to the edge of the brush and stood stamping his feet and shaking his horns.

Kenai rushed to meet Gus, tail whipping, barking a welcome. He danced wildly about the bear trying to entice him into playing. But play was beneath Gus's dignity. He scarcely noticed the dog.

Eric realized with a shock that Gus was no longer the

playful young bear who would spend hours romping with Kenai, the half-grown bear who had disappeared into the mountains alone for the first time last fall. Sometime during the winter and spring that clumsy, playful, immature Gus had disappeared. In his place emerged a Kodiak bear, big, powerful, sure of himself, with regal bearing and kingly dignity.

Ten-Day Watson studied the advancing Gus critically and said, "Didn't I tell you he'd be a bruiser? And he's not quite through growing yet."

Gus padded straight to Eric, thrust up his big black nose, and whoofed mightily. Eric patted his solid forehead and rubbed his stubby ears. Gus rumbled deep in his massive chest and pushed at Eric's hands searching for food. Eric said delightedly, "You remembered, Gus. You remembered."

"His stomach remembered," Watson said dryly.

"He remembered," Eric insisted and ran to the cabin for the leftover pancake, sugar cubes, and a bottle of sweetened water.

Ten-Day Watson watched as Gus deftly lifted sugar cubes and pieces of pancake from Eric's palm with a great chomping and smacking of lips. "He's yours all right. You're stuck with the big lug for as long as he lives."

Eric put his face down against Gus's broad nose and said, "We don't care, do we?"

Gus blew out a mighty breath and pushed at Eric's hands searching for more sweets.

In the following two weeks Eric saved six dollars from his wages. He hid them under the mattress of his bed. The other four had gone for a new shirt and sugar for Gus. He was thinking how he had almost half enough for the watch one night when he entered the house and found his father sitting at the table drinking a can of beer.

"Pa?" Eric said. "I thought you were fishing."

"Hit a rock and bent a propeller blade. Had to come in to straighten it. You still hangin' around that Crazy Watson?"

"He's not crazy," Eric said. "You want something to eat?"

"Had supper." His father finished the beer and wiped his

mouth with a palm. You helpin' with that placer minin' yet?"

"I've got nothing else to do."

"He don't have to buy milk or anything for that bear anymore so you've got no excuse to work for nothin'. From now on you get paid. He payin' you?"

"I eat lunch with him and sometimes supper. That's pay, sort of."

"You know what I mean."

"He's paying me five dollars a week."

"Five dollars! What, that old cheapskate?"

"I didn't want anything," Eric explained. "He insisted."

"Are you crazy? It costs to live. I been buyin' your clothes and grub for close on to fifteen years." Ned Strong shook his head angrily and glared at his son. "Well, it's better'n nothin'. How much has he paid you?"

"Ten dollars."

Ted Strong held out his hand. "Get it. A kid your size — it's time you learned what money is and started payin' some of your own keep. I been supportin' you for years and I'm gettin' tired of it."

"Do you want me to bring home some groceries and things with it?" Eric hedged.

"You don't fool me, kid." Ned Strong leveled a finger at Eric. "You're figurin' to hold out on me. I want that ten dollars here in my hand."

"I haven't got ten, Pa. I had to buy a shirt and sugar for Gus."

"How much you got?"

"Six dollars."

"Get it. Now."

Eric got the five and the one dollar bill from under his mattress and put them in his father's hand. "Sure ain't much," his father muttered, "but it'll help some. I want that five dollars every week right here on this table. Understand?"

"Pa, I need some to buy sugar cubes for Gus and some for clothes."

"You don't have to feed that bear sugar anymore."

"He won't come back if I don't have something sweet for him," Eric explained. "That's part of the reason I go up to Mr. Watson's."

"You can have a dollar a week. That'll buy all the sugar you'll need. I want the rest right here." He tapped the table-top. "Any clothes you need, I'll get."

The next morning Eric went past George Summers' store and didn't even glance at the window.

The activity at Watson's settled into its usual summer with but one exception. Gus wandered off on his own into the hills and valleys each day to hunt small game, roots, and herbs and to fish on a distant stream. He would come padding back across the tundra after some hours, head straight for Eric, and thrust up his big head to have his ears scratched. Eric mar-veled that he once held this great brute in his arms and saved him from starving. "How was the fishing?" he'd ask. "Did you catch any squirrels today?" Gus would rumble deep in his chest and push at Eric's hands searching for sweets.

This was how things were at Ten-Day Watson's until the day a great white ship sailed majestically across the bay and tied up at the long-deserted dock.

# - 4 -

IT WAS EARLY morning and Eric was on his way to Ten-Day Watson's. He had stopped at the window of George Summers' store to admire the gold wristwatch when the deep boom rolled over the town and died in echoes against the snow-laden hills. Eric looked toward the bay, and there, crossing the still blue water came a great white ship, heading straight for the empty dock.

Doors burst open along the street. People shouted and pointed. They began to race toward the dock. Eric ran with them. The whistle came again and dogs began barking. Eric heard over and over the glad cries, "A ship! Look, a ship! A ship?"

The whole town streamed onto the dock.

Joe Lucky was there jumping up and down like a scarecrow, waving a fish pole in one hand, a couple of fish on a string in the other, and shouting in a voice so high it almost broke. "A ship! I knew it'd come. I knew it. Oh, by golly, a ship at last?"

It was the first big ship Eric had ever seen. He stood transfixed as it edged up to the dock. Lines were thrown over and it was made fast. The side of the ship was lined with people looking down at them. Hands waved, voices called to them, "What town is this? Is the whole town here?"

"Including dogs and cats," someone laughed. A man in a blue uniform, wearing an officer's cap, gave orders. Golden letters along the side of the bow read *Northern Queen*.

A voice near Eric said, "Cruise ship heading north, I'd guess." Another said, "I've heard of her. Golden Nugget Line. They've got planes and ships both. Take you anyplace you want to go. Wonder why she stopped here?"

Someone called the question up to the ship, and a man leaning over said, "Burned out a main bearing. We'll be here about three days, they tell us, while they repack it."

A gangplank was run out and well-dressed people in sport clothes came down to the dock. They walked about, looking at the bay, the old town, the line of snowcapped mountains belting the horizon. Eric admired the ship. The people were dressed in clothes such as he'd never seen in this far northern village. He wanted to watch longer, but he had to tell Ten-Day Watson this marvelous news. He turned and ran up the gravel road.

"A big ship?" Ten-Day Watson waded ashore and stuck his shovel in the soft earth. "I wondered what made you so late. Now, wouldn't that beat all after twenty years? A cruise ship, you say."

Eric nodded. "There must have been two hundred people walking around on the dock when I left." He glanced about. Kenai was lying in front of the cabin in the sun. Gus and Sitka were not about.

"Well, them that always said a ship would come finally got one," Watson observed, "even if it is only for a few days." He took his shovel and waded back into the creek.

Eric got his boots from the cabin and joined the old man. For a time they worked steadily in companionable silence. Sitka appeared, and stood stripping leaves from a nearby bush. Finally Gus came padding across the distant tundra, swinging his big head and rolling his shoulders. He had finished his morning fishing on a distant creek. Now he made straight for Eric and his daily handout of sweets.

Eric waded ashore and went to the cabin with Gus at his heels. He put a handful of sugar cubes in his pocket and found a pancake Watson had left smothered in syrup. He gave Gus a sugar cube, waited until he'd eaten it, then tore the pancake into small pieces and let Gus lift each one delicately from his palm. He smiled at the velvety touch of Gus's soft lips. He patted the broad forehead and let Gus sniff both hands to make sure there was no more food. Then he went to join Ten-Day Watson in the creek again. Gus hunted a cool spot and flopped for his morning nap.

When Eric returned home that night, tourists were wandering the town's one street and dock, searching for some entertainment. A half dozen sat on a rickety bench before one of the vacant stores. They looked bored.

The same people were walking about the next morning when Eric headed for Watson's. They seemed at a loss for something to do while they waited for their ship to be repaired.

Eric and Ten-Day Watson had been working about an hour, and Gus and Kenai were napping nearby, when Joe Lucky came up the trail from the road with four people.

Kenai rose and went to confront them in the cabin's yard. They looked at his yellow eyes and wolflike head and stopped. They all wore bright sport clothes and carried cameras.

Eric said, "There's some people at the cabin."

"Seen 'em." Watson continued shoveling.

Eric waited a minute. "Hadn't we ought to ask what they want?"

"Know what they want," Watson said.

Eric began to feel uncomfortable with those people, confronted by Kenai, watching them. He was beginning to think he could stand it no longer when Watson waded ashore, stuck his shovel into the bank, and went toward them.

Eric followed.

Joe Lucky kept watching the dog. He said uneasily, "Ten-Day, these folks are off the ship. They'd like to see your tame Kodiak, and the deer, and how you mine gold. They've never seen any of these things."

Ten-Day Watson scowled at the four people and said nothing. Finally, the bigger of the men said, "We don't want to intrude, Mr. Watson. But now that we are here, would it be all right if I went over and took a picture of your bear while he's sleeping by that bush?"

"You stay here," Watson said. "Gus ain't used to anybody but Eric and me. Eric, get Gus up."

Eric went to the cabin and got more sugar cubes and approached the sleeping Gus. He leaned over and scratched his stubby ears. "Gus," he said, "get up." He held the sugar cube before the bear's nose. "Get up if you want it." Gus heaved to his feet and Eric gave him the cube. "These people came to see you," Eric said, patting the big head. Gus blinked at them, smacking his lips, black nose, the keenest in all the world, reaching for any stray scent. Eric held a second cube in his palm and walked a circle. Gus padded after him, reaching for the sugar, making grunting noises. Finally Eric let him have it. All four tourists kept aiming and shooting pictures. Eric leaned over and Gus sniffed at the boy's smiling face. He licked his hands to be sure there was nothing more, then went back to the cool spot to nap.

Sitka came out of the brush to investigate and the cameras turned on the deer. One of the women said, "Oh, my! Can we pet him?"

"He won't let you near," Watson said gruffly.

Kenai came in for attention. Now that Watson and Eric seemed on friendly terms with the strangers, he was. He sat on his tail, ran out his tongue, and grinned. He looked like the part wolf he was.

"Is it all right to pet him," the women asked.

"You can pet him," Watson said grudgingly.

"Can we see the sluice boxes, Ten-Day?" Joe Lucky asked.

"Is that what they used to get gold with?" one of the women asked. "How does it work?"

Watson led them up to the sluice boxes. When he said nothing, Joe Lucky explained how they trapped the gold.

"My grandfather panned gold in the north years ago," the smaller man said. "I'd sure like to try it, just for fun."

"You got a couple of pans around so the folks could try it — just for a while?" Joe Lucky asked hopefully.

Watson scowled and scratched at his beard, then he said, "Eric, get four of those pans outa the cabin."

The tourists tried their luck and the few grains they found Watson put into an envelope and gave them. They gravitated back to the napping Gus, took more pictures of him, thanked Watson and Eric profusely, and went down the trail with Joe Lucky.

Eric said, "They were nice. That was kind of fun, wasn't it?"

Watson grunted. "We lost almost an hour." He picked up his shovel and returned to the creek.

A half hour later Joe Lucky was back with four more tourists and it started all over again. This continued all forenoon and into the afternoon as fast as Lucky could return one group to town and pick up another. Finally Watson said bluntly, "No more, Joe. This's the last."

"Aw, now, Ten-Day," Lucky protested, "they only wanta look."

"Look someplace else. No more. It takes too much time."

"But, Ten-Day…"

Joe Lucky shrugged and left with his latest group.

Eric and Watson finished out the day with no further interruptions. Gus went to his distant creek to fish and returned for his evening handout of sweets. He lay in the yard in front of the cabin, pink tongue laboriously reaching for the last drop inside a syrup can. Eric and Watson had just finished supper when Joe Lucky returned. This time there was a tall, blue-uniformed man with him, Eddie Lang, who owned the town's only bar, and George Summers, who owned the grocery store.

Watson said, "Lucky, I told you…"

"Hold it," Joe Lucky said quickly. "This ain't a sightseein' trip. These ain't tourists. You know George Summers and Eddie Lang. And this here's Captain Nelson off the *Northern Queen*. Captain Nelson wants to talk to you."

Captain Nelson was all business. His voice was crisp and

33

authoritative. "I'd like to look around, Mr. Watson. Then I'd like to discuss a business matter with you. That is, if everything is as I've been told. If it isn't, I'll leave and you can forget I was here."

"What do you wanta see?" Watson asked.

"Everything you showed these people today. A bear, deer, a part-wolf dog, your sluice boxes and gold panning."

It took but a few minutes to show Captain Nelson everything. He asked no questions, but Eric could see the captain did not miss a word and his sharp eyes took in every detail. He returned to Gus a second time and stood looking at him. Gus glanced up, licked his lips, then returned to the syrup can.

When they were again in the cabin, Captain Nelson came right to the point. "The whole ship's buzzing about your bear, deer, and wolf dog. Those that panned a few grains of gold have shown them all over."

"What's this business you wanta talk about?" Watson asked.

"The Golden Nugget Line can use another stopping place along this coast. We had one south of here a day's run, but that earthquake, last winter, destroyed it. Passengers are anxious to get off the ship for a day or so after they've come this far. They'd like to look at the country, maybe see some game, get the feel of the great North. That's what we sell them on when they take this cruise.

"Now, looking at it through the tourist's eye, which we have to do, you have all the ingredients here to make this a worthwhile stopover spot. You've got the old town with its mining history, fine docking facilities, wonderful scenery, and an abandoned airport where cruise planes could land. Right here you have the prospector's cabin, a deer, a part-wolf dog, a placer-mining operation, and the old gold pans. These are musts in this kind of business. But they are not unusual. We can find this setup a dozen places along the coast. But you do have one thing that makes this place more desirable than any of the others." He pointed through the door where Gus was still working on the empty syrup can.

"Gloomy Gus?" Watson said.

"Gloomy Gus. Ninety percent of the people who come north on these cruises have read about or heard about Alaska's giant Kodiak bears. They all want to see one, but practically none of them ever will. In five years this is my first sight of one. The word 'bear' does something to people's minds that nothing else can. They immediately begin conjuring up the most amazing images of savage, prehistoric beasts coming out of dark cave mouths. There's a fascination to bears that no other animal can equal. To be able to come up here and see this bear, as some folks did today, has made the whole trip for them. They can go home and say they stood within a few feet of a giant Kodiak bear, the biggest meat-eater on earth. And most of them will have the pictures to prove it. Now, then, Mr. Watson, if you can guarantee that when we bring people up here they'll see all that they did today, especially that bear of yours, I'll recommend to the company that we make this a regular stop."

"Gus belongs to Eric," Watson said.

Captain Nelson turned to Eric. "What do you say, son?"

"I wouldn't mind," Eric said uncertainly, "if it's all right with Mr. Watson."

"Well, it's not," Watson said promptly.

"But, Ten-Day?" George Summers adjusted his gold-rimmed glasses. "This is a chance for Tatouche to come back, to be something again. Think of it."

"Not interested. Eric and me can't spend all day long showing people around."

"Naturally you'd be paid," Eddie Lang said.

"You people will have to settle that," Captain Nelson said.

"All right," Joe Lucky offered, "I'll pay Eric twenty-five cents a head for everybody I bring up here to see his bear. He won't have to do a thing but collect."

"That don't take care of Ten-Day," Eddie Lang pointed out. "He's got to be paid."

"Then you fellers pay him. Let the town chip in," Joe

Lucky said. "I'm payin' Eric."

"Darned little," Eddie Lang said. "Captain, how is it usually done?"

"What the tourist pays in one lump sum should take care of it. That is, if it's a sizable amount."

"How much you charging to haul those people up here two miles?" George Summers asked.

"It's four miles," Joe Lucky said. "I got to haul 'em back."

"How much?" Summers demanded.

"Two-fifty. But I got to buy tires and gas. I got to keep the car runnin'. Besides, it was my idea to bring those people up here to start with."

"Forget it?" Watson said. "I don't want a lot of people tramping over the country. Next thing they'll be tearing it up, driving out the game, just like they did before. Won't be fit to live in again."

"Did these people cause any trouble today?" Captain Nelson asked. "Did they destroy or damage anything?"

"They was all right," Watson said grudgingly.

"They'll all be the same," Captain Nelson explained. "These are tourists on vacation. Each group would be around here less than an hour. They want to see the country, the game, whatever you have to show them. They aren't interested in destroying, and we certainly aren't. We sell the beauty of the North scenery. If any of it is ruined, we're out of business. We want Tatouche to stay as it is. Oh, open a couple of the old buildings for restaurants, a small hotel, some novelty shops and such. But leave the town as it is. If the town and country go modern, we won't stop anymore. It will have lost the romance of the North, the Gold Rush era, our last frontier. Personally, I should think you'd be proud of what you have here, Mr. Watson, and enjoy showing it to people who have never seen such things and probably never will again."

Ten-Day Watson scratched his white beard thoughtfully. Then he looked at Eric. "You wanta to do this, eh?"

"I'd kind of like to — if you would," Eric said.

Ten-Day Watson took off his hat and dug thick fingers

through his white hair. He kept looking at Eric, then he looked out the door at Gus who'd lost interest in the syrup can and was wandering off into the pale northern gloom. "How many ships and planes will be coming in here?" he asked.

"Ship a week all summer and fall. Two planes a week with from thirty to fifty passengers each."

Watson shook his head. "We wouldn't have time to take out any dust. And all these people will want to pan some gold. They'll be taking out what I should be getting for my winter's stake. I'd have to get my money from the tourists somehow." He looked at Joe Lucky. "I want a dollar a head. With what Eric takes leaves you a dollar and a quarter. I figure that's fair."

"That's half." Joe Lucky's voice climbed into a squeak. "You're crazy."

"Then forget it," Watson shrugged. "We've got work to do."

"Hold on a minute," Eddie Lang soothed. "We can figure something out."

"Sure," Joe Lucky said. "Ten-Day don't own all this land, just where the cabin is and a little bit on the creek. I can bring people up here and we can stand right out there on the trail and watch, and you can't stop us, Ten-Day."

"Won't try," Watson said mildly.

"We can see ever' thing we did today." Joe Lucky looked from Summers to Lang. "We got nothin' to worry about."

"Not quite everything," Watson said. "Gus likely won't be here. He goes fishing a lot. He's here mostly because we coax him back."

"We need that bear," Captain Nelson said quickly. "He's the key to the whole thing. We've got to have the bear."

"I know you need to be paid," Summers said to Watson. "I'll ask around. Maybe we can help a little but we haven't much money."

"If Mr. Lucky can't make it on a dollar and a quarter a head," Captain Nelson said, "I can bring in another man who'll be glad to take it on that basis."

37

"Now, wait a minute," Joe Lucky began.

"Good," Eddie Lang said. "How soon can you get him here?"

Joe Lucky fidgeted uncomfortably. "All right," he threw up his hands, "I'll give Ten-Day the dollar and Eric a quarter. But it ain't fair, I can tell you that. It ain't fair."

"Good, we've got that settled," Captain Nelson said. "Now, we need some way to get more people up here each trip. Isn't there a bus around?"

"There's an old one been sittin' out in the hangar at the airfield for five years," Joe Lucky said. "It was runnin' good when they left it. It'll carry about forty people. The battery and points are likely shot now."

"I'll send up a pair of mechanics with a battery," Captain Nelson said. "They can have it running by morning. One other thing — you'll have to put a chain on Gloomy Gus when the tourists are around."

"But he's tame," Eric insisted. "He's never been tied. He won't do anything."

"I know," Captain Nelson smiled. "But with tourists around we have to be extra careful. And another thing — do you have enough gold pans, Mr. Watson?"

"I've got eight."

"I must have a hundred stashed away in the back room," Eddie Lang said. "I'll send some up in the morning."

"Then we're in business, gentlemen." Captain Nelson rose. "Be sure to have Gloomy Gus here and give the tourists a good show."

After they'd gone Eric said, "You don't like it, do you?"

"We didn't have any choice. Joe Lucky can bring tourists up here, just like he said. They could stand around and see everything, including Gloomy Gus. That bear'll keep coming around whether we coax him or not. But I don't mind showing what we got. Those were nice folks today and they did just come to look. I guess you, me, and Gus, and Kenai and Sitka are gonna be in the entertainment business. Sort of." He rose and looked in the cracked mirror, turning his head, studying it. "Was gonna cut some of this beard off this summer. My hair, too. Guess I won't now. Just even her up a little. Looks more like a hairy old prospector's supposed to. You need a haircut, though. I'll cut yours, then you can cut mine."

Gus padded to the open door and thrust his big head inside. He sniffed loudly, searching for some scent of food. Ten-Day Watson leveled a finger at him accusingly and said, "It's all your fault, you gloomy cuss."

Next morning, when Joe Lucky led the first busload of tourists up the trail, they were ready. They had moved the sluice boxes close to shore so people could see inside. The gold pans were set out in a row on the creek bank, each with a shovel full of gravel. Kenai went to meet them, tail waving. Sitka stayed near the brush, stamping his small feet and flapping his big ears. Gus squatted at the base of a tree, and for the first time he was chained. But he didn't seem to mind. He was busy cleaning up the last of a batch of pancakes that had been prepared especially for him.

Ten-Day Watson had worked out a spiel. He stood before the crowd in front of the cabin and said, "I'm Ten-Day Watson. The dog's Kenai; he's part wolf. The deer's name is Sitka, 'cause he's a Sitka blacktail. That's Eric Strong with his bear, Gloomy Gus. He's the only tame Kodiak in the world." From there on the spiel was all Gus. "Eric found him when he was just a little-bitty cub about so long. We hand-raised him on milk and pieces of salmon and pancakes with syrup."

"I thought bears were meat-eaters, like cats," a woman said.

"They're meat-eaters," Watson agreed, "but their favorite food is berries, roots, and grass, and salmon when the spawning run is on. Most of the meat they eat is small rodents like mice and ground squirrels."

"How tame is he now?" someone asked.

Watson said, "Eric, show the folks how tame Gus is."

Eric scratched Gus's ears and under his chin. He held a sugar cube under his nose and said, "If you want it, get up." Gus heaved to his feet and stood eating the cube while cameras whirred and clicked, and people "Oh'd and Ah'd" at his size. Eric held a second cube in his palm and walked a small circle with Gus pacing at his heels grunting and reaching for the cube. The people were amazed and delighted. Sitka and Kenai came in for pictures, too. The dog stood among them, waving his tail, happy at being noticed. Sitka kept his distance, snorting delicately and stamping his feet. Then the tourists tried their hand at panning gold. Ten-Day Watson walked around them helping and instructing. When they finished, they gravitated back for a final look and more picture-taking of Gus. Then they went down the trail with Joe Lucky carrying their few grains of gold, talking about a tame deer, a part-wolf dog, and especially about a tame Kodiak bear.

Days passed. The ship was repaired and all three hundred passengers had been out to the little cabin on Friday Creek. The night the ship left Joe Lucky came up and gave Watson their money. After he'd gone they sat at the table and the old man divided it. "There you are," he said to Eric. "You got seventy-five dollars for letting people look at old Gloomy Gus. Bet you never thought he'd earn you that kind of money."

"No." Eric fingered the small roll of bills. He'd never had so much money in all his life.

"You know, come fall," Watson said, "you might have as much as seven or eight hundred dollars. What're you going to do with all that money?"

Eric smiled thoughtfully, ruffling the bills. "There's a gold wristwatch with a leather band in George Summer's window. The hands and figures have that stuff on so you can see it at night. It's been there an awful long time. It's $14.98." He drew a deep breath and looked at Ten-Day Watson, his gray eyes shining. "I'm going to buy that watch," he said in a low voice. "Can I leave the rest with you?"

"I'll keep track of it and put it away with mine."

They were still sitting there smiling at each other when Eric's father walked in. He looked at them and the money on the table. He licked his lips and rubbed a hand across his

40

mouth. Eric felt sick just looking at him.

"Heard about that cruise ship and what you been doin' up here," he said to Eric. "Joe Lucky says he gives you a quarter a head for every person he brings up; and he brought around three hundred." He pointed at the pile of bills before Eric. "That the money?"

"Yes," Eric said.

Ned Strong reached over and gathered up the bills.

"Just a minute," Watson said, "that's Eric's money."

"I'll take care of it for 'im."

"I know how you'll take care of it," Watson said angrily.

"How I do is my business. He's my kid."

"You can at least leave him enough to buy that wrist-watch in George Summer's window that he wants."

"What's he want with a watch?" Ned Strong stuffed the bills in his pocket. "Lucky says you get a dollar a head for the people comin' up here and that dumb bear is what's bringin' 'em. I'll take half that dollar for the bear's part." He reached for the pile of bills before Ten-Day Watson.

The old man's fist shot out with a speed that surprised Eric, and closed on his father's hand. Eric saw the muscles bulge in the thick wrist, then turn the hand over and deftly pluck the bills from the fingers. Watson's deep-blue eyes looked steadily into his father's surprised bloodshot ones. Then his father looked away. "I wouldn't ever try that again," Watson said quietly. He let go of the hand, and Eric's father backed away rubbing his wrist.

"I want that twenty-five cents the kid gets," his father said, "or he don't come up here no more."

"You'll get it, if Eric says so."

Eric looked at the tabletop and murmured, "He can have it."

"I want it every Saturday night and no cheatin' me."

"You'll get it, and don't say that again."

"All right. All right." Eric's father backed to the door. "You get home," he said to the boy. "You hear me?" Then he was gone.

Watson said, "I had to give it to him, you being his son and all. I'm sorry."

"I guess I wouldn't have known what to do with so much money anyway," Eric said.

Ten-Day Watson put bills before him. "Get your watch, son."

Eric shook his head. "I wanted to earn it."

"You earned it ten times over."

"I wanted to buy it with my own money." Eric pushed back the chair. He felt tired and letdown. "I guess I'd better go home."

He walked out and started down the dim trail. Off across the shadowy tundra Gus's black shape was heading for his favorite fishing stream.

# - 5 -

CAPTAIN NELSON'S promise came true. The first of each week a cruise ship sailed across the bay and tied up at the dock. Twice a week, planes landed at the old airstrip bringing more tourists. Once again there was the sound of feet tramping the old wooden sidewalks, the bustle of people moving about. Carefree laughter and talk rang in the street. The ancient bus, with Joe Lucky at the wheel, was kept busy shuttling from the airfield to town and from town up to Ten-Day Watson's.

Amazing things began happening to Tatouche. George Summers started repairs to open one of the old restaurants that had been closed for years. Next door to the restaurant a new man in town added windows, repaired the front door of a building, and opened a camera shop. Across the street a curio and artifacts store opened. It displayed Eskimo carving, gold nuggets, Indian and Eskimo beadwork, and handmade clothing. A man flew in by plane one day and began tearing the boards off the boarded-up windows of the old Copper Lady saloon. Soon people were again entering the ancient swinging doors for beer, soft drinks, and sandwiches. The altar was let down from the ceiling by ropes, and a man lectured on the past of Tatouche, particularly about the Copper Lady, while the tourists drank from the mugs which had once collected the Sunday church offering. A guide moved in with a dozen horses, knocked out the partitions of a couple of the old houses and used them for barns. He began taking people for horseback rides showing them the glaciers and the country.

Ted Benjamin, who had worked in the mine years ago, repaired an old speeder, a handcar powered by a gasoline engine, the mine officials had used. It would carry a dozen passengers. He took tourists up to view the old mine shafts and buildings and the mountains of rusting machinery.

Day and night the sounds of saws and hammers were heard. In an amazingly short time Tatouche's one-block business district had grown into two. Overnight, old forgotten Tatouche had become a tourist attraction. The center of interest was a huge Kodiak bear named Gus.

A cameraman arrived and took pictures of Eric and Gus. These were displayed in ads by the Golden Nugget Line.

Eric's father had benefited from the influx of tourists. He had quit fishing and now spent nearly all his time in the bar with his two friends. He came home only occasionally to sleep. Every Saturday, when Joe Lucky paid Eric and Ten-Day Watson their share, he was there to collect all that Gloomy Gus and the boy had earned. Ten-Day Watson grumbled about it, but Eric didn't mind too much. He was with the old man, his one friend, and Gus, the only living thing he'd ever loved and owned. He enjoyed meeting the people. And Gus seemed to enjoy it, too. The tourists brought the bear pieces of cake, and shared cookies, sandwiches, and candy bars with him. These they gave to Eric and watched, fascinated, as Gus daintily lifted each morsel from the boy's palm. A few of the braver souls offered the tidbits themselves and were delighted at the touch of Gus's soft lips.

Gus was looking for food now. The moment he heard the old bus motor down on the road he was up and straining at the end of his chain, waiting, licking his lips in anticipation, black nose questing eagerly for the first scent of food.

"Look at him," Watson said. "By fall he'll be fat as a pig. Wild horses couldn't drag him away now because this is where the big handouts are." But late each afternoon after the tourists had gone they turned Gus loose and he went padding across the tundra to the distant stream to fish for salmon. In

44

the morning he was back, looking for the sweets he knew would be there. He did not object to being chained as long as he was so well fed.

The summer passed. The last planeload of tourists flew in and departed. The last cruise ship was due. The salmon run was long since over. Migratory fowl had winged their way south, and the snow line had crept to the edge of the tundra where it awaited the first blast of winter. Gus was rolling fat. He would soon be heading into the mountains for his winter sleep. Approaching winter was snipping the daylight hours away at a rate of seven minutes a day.

The last cruise ship tied up at the dock. With the passengers that streamed down the gangplank came a short, fat bald man. He had sharp, black eyes set close together and a round, small mouth. He was followed by a black-haired, stocky boy. The two made straight for Joe Lucky standing beside the old bus. "This the bus that takes people up to see that tame Kodiak bear?" the man asked.

"Gloomy Gus?" Joe Lucky nodded. "Just as soon as we get a load we'll be off. Climb aboard."

The fat man wasn't through asking questions yet. "I hear the bear's tame?"

"He was bottle-raised. Eric found him on the tundra when he wasn't no bigger'n that."

"They say he's the only tame Kodiak in the world."

"Far as we know, he is."

"Anybody can pet him?" the boy asked.

"Eric and Watson do. A few tourists do, too. Most are afraid of him. He's so big."

The bus began filling and the boy and fat man got aboard.

At Watson's the two of them paid no attention to the gold panning or to Kenai or Sitka. They headed for Gus and stood just beyond the chain's length studying him. They watched as Gus ate from Eric's hand and followed him around reaching for the sugar cube. They took no pictures. When the rest of the crowd wandered off to other interests, they stayed.

The fat man asked, "You the kid that raised him?"

"Yes, sir," Eric said.

"He's a genuine Kodiak?" The man's sharp, doubtful voice aroused Eric's antagonism.

Eric nodded, "He's a Kodiak."

"You sure he's the only tame one in the world?"

"Captain Nelson says he is. They don't live anyplace but up here and no Alaskan has ever seen a tame one before."

"Can he do any tricks?" the boy asked.

"Just what you saw."

"Following you around is no trick," the boy said scornfully.

"He's big all right," the fat man observed. "Biggest bear I ever saw."

"But dumb," the boy said. "And he's still got his claws and those big tearing teeth. Why don't you pull his claws and knock out those teeth?" he asked Eric.

"Why?" Eric asked, shocked.

"So you can teach him tricks, so you can handle him. It's too dangerous messing around a bear, unless he's declawed and those big teeth are out and he's muzzled."

"I don't want to teach him tricks," Eric said, scratching Gus's ears.

The boy turned away disdainfully. "A bear that can't do tricks is no good."

"Is he tame enough for anybody to be around?" the fat man asked.

"Some of the tourists pet him and feed him things." Eric put an arm around his neck and Gus tilted his big nose and sniffed loudly at the boy. "We only have him chained because Captain Nelson said to. When we're alone he's not chained."

"I see."

The crowd drifted back from their gold panning for one last look at Gus before they left. Cameras clicked and whirred again as they stood about watching Eric pet Gus and feed him by hand.

The fat man approached Watson. "You the boy's pa?"

46

"His pa's in town."

"An uncle then?"

Watson shook his head. "My name's Watson, his is Strong. We're sort of partners, you might say."

The fat man nodded and called to the boy, "Come on, Cliff." They went down the trail to the bus ahead of the rest of the tourists.

In Tatouche the fat man asked Joe Lucky, "Where will I find Mr. Strong?"

"Ned Strong?" Lucky laughed. "Go down to Eddie Lang's bar. He's practically bought a stool there."

The fat man and the boy went into Eddie Lang's, but the people there were all tourists.

Eddie came down the bar and the fat man asked, "Where will I find Ned Strong?"

"Probably home sleeping one off," Eddie Lang said. "He ain't been in since early this morning. Go to the end of this street. There you'll see a double row of old, empty shacks. His is the last one. You can't miss it. It's the only one being lived in."

They found the old house and stood in the weed-infested yard looking at the closed door. A dirty, torn curtain hung across the door's window. No smoke issued from the rusty stovepipe.

"Maybe he's not home," Cliff studied the old shack. "Must be some kind of a nut living like this."

"We've come all this way. I'm going to see." The fat man went up the rickety steps and hammered on the door. There was no answer. He tried the knob and found it unlocked. Carefully he pushed the door open. "Mr. Strong," he called. "Mr. Strong." As the door swung wider the light entered the room and they saw inside. A short, stocky man lay sprawled on his back on a bunk snoring noisily.

The fat man and Cliff walked in and looked down at the man. "Sleeping one off, all right," the fat man said. "I got a feeling this's good." He shook Ned Strong's shoulder and said, "Mr. Strong, wake up." He kept shaking Ned Strong's shoulder and talking to him.

Ned Strong finally roused and mumbled, "Huh? What's that? That you, kid?"

"He's out," Cliff said. "You won't get anything from him."

"We've got to," the fat man said. "Is there coffee in that pot on the stove?"

"It's half full."

"Light a fire and get it hot."

A few minutes later the fat man and Cliff lifted Ned Strong to the edge of the bed. While the boy held him upright, the fat man cramped Strong's slack fingers around the hot cup and ordered, "Drink it, Mr. Strong. Drink it all. We've got to talk to you. Do you understand? We've got to talk to you."

It took more than an hour of talking, coaxing, and bullying and all the coffee in the pot before Ned Strong could get groggily to his feet, stumble to the washbasin, and slosh cold water over his face and neck. The cold water helped. In a few more minutes he appeared reasonably sober. He looked at the two people sitting at the table and scowled. "What're you doin' waking a man up in the middle of the day? Who're you, anyway?"

The fat man smiled and said, "If you'll sit down and listen, Mr. Strong, I'll explain. We've come more than two thousand miles to talk to you."

"That so? Two thousand miles, huh?" He rubbed his hand uncertainly over his face, walked to the chair, and sat down heavily. "What do you wanta see me about?"

The fat man placed a card before Ned Strong. Strong squinted at it. He rubbed his eyes and held the card close. Finally he handed it back. "Light's bad."

The fat man picked up the card and read, "Henry D. Marcel and Son. Continental Circus. I'm Henry D. Marcel. This is my son, Cliff."

"Circus! What's a circus doin' way up here?"

"We didn't bring our circus," Henry Marcel explained patiently. "We came to see you."

"Don't know nothin' 'bout circuses.

"We're interested in that bear of your son's. What's his name, Gloomy Gus? We'd like to add him to our circus."

"You mean buy him?"

"We're prepared to pay you three hundred dollars for him?"

"That all?" Ned Strong's mind was becoming clearer. "He makes more'n that in a month with folks payin' to see 'im. Why, that Gloomy Gus is a gold mine."

"But that only lasts three months out of the year," Mr. Marcel said.

"I been worryin' about that some," Strong said gloomily.

"Tell you what, Mr. Strong. I'll double my offer. Six hundred. That's a mighty good price for an untrained bear. Six hundred will tide you over the winter," he added shrewdly.

Ned Strong scowled. Then he shook his head. "Gus would be gone for good. We wouldn't have a bear for next year. Why, that Gus is good for another twenty years. And next season I'll make 'em jack up the price. No, sir, that Gloomy Gus ain't for sale. Not now, not ever. People're gonna want to see him more every year. Only tame Kodiak in the world and don't you forget it."

"I see." Henry Marcel scratched his bald head. "All right, Mr. Strong. I'll lay my cards on the table. I can see you're a sharp businessman. I'm going to make you an offer you can't turn down. I can't really afford to do this, but we want that bear. I'll give you a hundred dollars a week, every week in the year for the use of Gloomy Gus."

"Gus don't go unless Eric and me are along. I own that bear, remember?"

"You'll still own him. That's five thousand two hundred dollars a year and neither you nor the boy will have to lift a hand. Just collect your hundred every week."

"You mean Eric won't have to mess with Gus? But then who…?"

"Another trainer will take over."

"Me," Cliff Marcel said. "I'm building a bear act. I'm already handling a couple of blacks. I might as well add yours to it. We'll teach him some tricks, like riding a motorcycle, balancing on a ball. Things like that. We'll pull his claws and knock out those big tearing teeth, too."

"Knock out his teeth?"

"They do it all the time," Henry Marcel explained. "It makes them easier to handle. Just those big tearing ones in front. A performing bear's got no use for tearing teeth and claws."

"He's a bear," Cliff Marcel pointed out. "No sense taking chances getting clawed up or bit. You can't trust a bear."

Ned Strong nodded. "Kid won't like it, though. And he won't wanta leave here."

"You're his father, aren't you?" Henry Marcel asked.

"What's that supposed to mean?" Ned Strong scowled.

"He's a minor. Makes no difference what he wants. You say 'go,' he goes."

"Yeah, sure," Ned Strong agreed.

"A hundred dollars a week, every week, cash. It's pretty good when you don't have to lift a hand to get it," Henry Marcel said. "How about it, Mr. Strong?"

Ned Strong fidgeted uncomfortably. "Well, now, it's gonna cost to live down there. Clothes and things," he said vaguely. "And like I said, I'll make 'em pay more to see Gus next year."

Henry Marcel glanced at his son and drummed short, fat fingers on the tabletop thoughtfully. Finally he said, "You drive a hard bargain, Mr. Strong. I guess I'll have to tell you the whole story. If you appear in the Henry D. Marcel and Son Circus, you'll probably be seen by the people of the big circuses. If you are, they'll likely offer you a lot more money to bring the only tame Kodiak in the world to their show."

"You mean one of them big outfits that's got hundreds of animals and lots of tents and things?"

"That's it."

"There's a chance we might get in there, huh?"

"A very good one. They're going to want your bear just

as we do. He's a great drawing card. Look what he did for Ta-touche this summer. Naturally I won't want to lose him, but I know it can't be helped eventually. I can't match the money those big shows pay. But during the time you're with us we'll make money showing the only tame Kodiak in the world."

"How much will one of them big outfits pay?" Strong asked eagerly.

Henry Marcel spread his small hands. "It could be any-where from two-fifty to five hundred a week. It depends on how good a bargainer you are."

Ned Strong straightened. "Made you tell me about those big shows, didn't I? Five hundred, you say?"

"It's possible. But there's more possibilities than just the circus business," Henry Marcel pointed out. "Once that bear is trained and he gets well known, there's also the picture busi-ness."

"What's that mean?"

"Hollywood, man. They make a lot of movies with ani-mal actors. Suppose they make one that calls for a big bear. What bear do you suppose they'll try to get?" Henry Marcel tapped Ned Strong's knee for emphasis. "Why, the only tame Kodiak in the world, naturally."

Ned Strong rubbed his chin thoughtfully. "You pay for shippin' Gus, the kid, and me to Seattle."

"I'll pay all the transportation charges," Henry Marcel agreed. "But I'll have to get yours and the boy's back. I'm not a rich man. And I'm really giving you a break, as you can see. I'll take out fifty dollars a week from the hundred until your transportation's paid. Then you get your hundred again. All right?"

Ned Strong nodded. "How do you figure to get the bear down there?"

"We'll have a cage built on the dock. It'll be up to you and the boy to get the bear into it. We've contacted a fishing boat that will put in here in a couple of days. They'll load the bear on board and head out to sea. There they'll stop a freighter coming from Anchorage. The bear and cage will be transferred aboard and shipped down to the dock in Seattle."

"You figured you'd get him all along, huh?"

"No," Henry Marcel smiled, "but I hoped and prepared just in case." He drew a paper from his pocket and unfolded it on the table. "Then it's agreed. While you're waiting for a bigger offer, your bear will work for the Henry D. Marcel and Son Continental Circus for one hundred a week."

Ned Strong pointed at the paper. "What's that?"

"A contract for your protection and mine."

Ned Strong scowled and Henry Marcel hurried on. "With this I can't back out on you. It insures your hundred a week. By the same token I'm assured of your bear for one year. I'm going to have to spend a lot of money on newspaper advertising, billboards, handbills, television, and radio. It helps protect the money I'll have to put out to advertise your bear."

"No contract," Ned Strong said.

"We need some assurance that you'll come, and that you'll stay with us for a while."

"I ain't passin' up that five hundred a week, and I ain't forgettin' about that movie thing either. You bet, I'll come. How long do you figure it'll take for one of them big outfits to learn about Gus?"

"A year, I'd guess."

"Then you got your year," Ned Strong said.

"I see." Henry Marcel studied Ned Strong's bloated face. He finally folded up the contract and returned it to his pocket. "All right, Mr. Strong. I guess we'll have to take you at your word. We'll go down and order the cage built."

"You do that?" Ned Strong rubbed his face thoughtfully. "Gonna be a surprise to the kid. Yes, sir, a real surprise."

# - 6 -

WHEN ERIC returned home that night, he was surprised to find his father there and moderately sober.

For the first time his father asked, "How'd it go? You have many people up there to see Gus?"

"We had ninety," Eric said.

"That all?"

"My share came to twenty-two fifty."

"Chicken feed," his father said. "What'd you say if I told you that bear was gonna make us a hundred dollars a week every week in the year? And after the first year, five hundred a week, maybe even more. What'd you say to that?"

"What're you talking about, Pa? This is the last cruise ship until spring and the planes are all through. The season never lasts more than three months. And anyway Gus will be heading into the mountains soon for his winter sleep."

"Not this year," his father grinned. "We're goin' south; you and Gus and me."

"What do you mean, going south?"

"Man was here today, him and his son. They came two thousand miles to see me about that Gus." Eric stood dumbfounded while his father told him about Henry D. Marcel and his son and the Continental Circus; the hundred dollars a week they'd get the year around; the chance to go with one of the really big shows. "Five hundred a week they'll pay us, maybe more. We'll travel in style, see the whole country, live like kings, and all on account of that bear, that

Gloomy Gus. You won't have to do a thing. His kid'll take over handlin' Gus. What do you think of that, kid?"

Eric kept shaking his head. "We can't. We can't leave here. We can't take Gus away just to become a performing bear in somebody's circus."

"He's performing now," his father pointed out.

"This is different. This is his home. The people come to see him. After they're gone we turn him loose. He can go down to the creek to fish or into the meadows for mice and squirrels or do anything he likes. He's free, Pa. In a circus he'll be in a cage all the time and will only get out to perform. It's not right. This is Gus's home." He thought of something else and added, "Did they tell you they'd pull his claws and knock out those big teeth, too?"

"He's just a dumb bear. What difference does it make what they do to him?"

"It makes a lot of difference." For the first time Eric was standing up to his father. He was fighting for Gus with everything he had. "What about Mr. Watson? The tourists go up there expecting to see Gus. He's the big attraction. It might ruin Mr. Watson. And what about Tatouche? Captain Nelson said the whole thing was off this spring if Gus wouldn't be here. People want to see him more than anything else. Without Gus maybe the ships and planes won't stop anymore. Then what happens to the town, Pa? Captain Nelson said..."

"Don't care about Captain Nelson. Don't care about Crazy Watson, don't care about this town. Why should I? Why should you? What did any of 'em ever do for you and me? You got to look out for yourself in this world. That's what we're gonna do, kid. We're gonna live like kings. Yes-siree-Bob, like kings."

Eric saw he was getting nowhere and tried another tack. "I don't want to go, Pa. This is home, yours and mine. I don't want to go down there and live among a lot of strangers in some circus. I want to live here."

His father looked around. "In this shack? It's 'most ready to fall down. In a couple more years it will."

"We can fix it up, Pa. I'll fix it up."

"Nothing doin'. This is the one chance we got to shake the dust of this place and we're doin' it."

"But, Pa, listen..."

"No more arguments. We're goin', and that's it." His father went to the shelf, got a can of beer, punched a hole in the top, and sat down to enjoy it, smiling at the thought of what lay ahead.

Eric backed to the door, opened it, and went out. He started running through town to Ten-Day Watson's. The street was lit by splashes of light from store windows. Tourists trooped in and out of the different buildings. The cruise ship was a blaze of light that bathed the deck. Eric thought of leaving his one friend, Ten-Day Watson, leaving Kenai and Sitka, leaving the North. He thought of Gus in a cage, looking out between bars the rest of his life, never again seeing this country he loved, never being free. When Eric finally turned up the trail to the cabin, he was painfully out of breath.

Kenai came to meet him waving his tail. His running had startled Sitka. The deer trotted to the edge of the brush, stopped, and looked back.

Ten-Day Watson sat at the table under the glow of a hurricane lamp mending a shirt. He looked up and asked, "Well, what brings you back this time of night?"

"Pa says we're leaving here and taking Gus along," Eric panted. "That little fat, bald man this morning was a circus man. He's offered Pa a hundred dollars a week to take Gus down to join his circus."

Watson put the needle and shirt carefully on the tabletop and said, "What's that! Sit down, Eric. Get your breath and begin at the beginning."

Eric raced through the story and Ten-Day Watson sat, big hands folded on the tabletop, and listened. When Eric finished, he scratched thoughtfully at his beard and muttered, "Hmmmm, hmmmm."

"What're we going to do, Ten-Day?" Eric asked frantically. "I can't leave you and Kenai and Sitka. You're the only friends I've ever had. This is the only real home I've ever known. I can't take Gus away. You know how it'll be with him caged. They'll pull his claws and knock out his teeth, too. They said so. And what's going to happen here if Gus leaves? We can't."

Watson scowled at the tabletop, his blue eyes thoughtful. "You say your pa was sober?" he asked finally.

"He was drinking a can of beer when I left."

"Then we can still talk to him. I been thinking. I've got about two thousand cash for this summer. All your pa wants is money. Maybe that much cash will look bigger to him than a hundred a week that he hasn't got yet."

"But that's your winter stake."

Ten-Day Watson smiled. "I'll make out. If it'll keep you and Gus here, he's welcome to it." He went to a drawer and took out a thick sheaf of bills. "Come on, let's talk to him while he's still sober enough to understand."

Eric's father sat at the table in their cabin. There were two empty beer cans before him and he held a third. Watson pulled up a chair, sat down at the table, and looked at him. Ned Strong finished his drink, wiped his mouth, and said, "What brings you down here, Ten-Day?" Then he held up a hand and said gravely, "Let me guess." He looked at Eric. "So you couldn't keep your mouth shut." He turned to Watson. "What do you think of it? A hundred bucks a week every week in the year and I don't have to turn a hand to get it. That's better'n you do on that piddlin' little claim."

Watson nodded. "It's better."

"Better'n you did all summer too, lettin' people stomp all over your place."

"It is, if you get it."

"What do you mean, if I get it?"

"How much do you know about this Henry D. Marcel and his circus?"

"Know that he's got a circus, that he's guaranteed me a hundred a week to show off that Gus bear."

"Just because he showed you a poster or a card and told

56

you he has a circus doesn't mean he's got one. Or, if he has, that it's any good."

"He's got one, all right," Ned Strong said confidently, "and big enough to guarantee me a hundred a week."

"What kind of guarantee?"

"It's a guarantee, all right. And that ain't all. The minute one of them big shows sees Gus they'll want him. And then I'll get five hundred. What do you think of that?"

"Suppose you get there and you don't get the hundred or the five hundred. You'll be a long way from home and broke. Ever think of that?"

"You'd like that, wouldn't you?"

"I don't care a hang about you. I'm thinking of Gus and Eric."

"I'll take care of them."

"Like you always have?" Watson asked angrily.

"Kid's never gone hungry," Ned Strong said stiffly. "He's got clothes on his back and a roof over his head. I'll tell you what's worryin' you. When I take Gus away, people won't be comin' up to your place just to see a dog and a deer, a couple of sluice boxes, and try to do a little gold pannin'. It's the bear that's been draggin' people up there and we both know it. With him gone you lose your soft touch. Right?"

"Gus is the big attraction," Watson agreed. "He always has been. But I got along before and I will again. I'm thinking of Gus and Eric being stranded down south. You've got no real proof this so-called circus man has anything. Tell you what, Ned," — Watson drew the roll of bills from his pocket and held it in his fist; Eric noticed how his father's eyes clung greedily to it." Maybe this deal down south will work out. Maybe it won't. A bird in the hand is worth two in the bush, any day." He began stacking the bills before Eric's father one at a time. "There's two thousand cash money to leave Eric and Gus here. That's more than you ever had before to see you through the winter. Next spring the cruise ships and planes will be coming again. We'll raise that twenty-five cents to see Gus to fifty. That'll give you double the money you made this summer. Man, you've got a sure thing here. Don't throw it away for something you know nothing about."

Eric held his breath and waited. He didn't see how his father could resist. He picked up the pile of bills and counted them carefully. "Two thousand, all right."

"Two thousand sure dollars."

"Sure enough is." He fingered the bills. He rubbed a hand across his face and sighed gustily. Then he laid the pile down carefully and shoved them in front of Watson. "Keep your chicken feed," he said. "Soon as one of them big shows sees us we'll make that much in a month."

"You think so?"

"I got the only tame Kodiak in the world. Everybody'll want 'im. Day after tomorrow mornin' we pull out."

"I see." Ten-Day Watson folded the bills carefully and returned them to his pocket. "I guess that's about it," he said to Eric and walked outside.

Eric followed and closed the door. "Ten-Day," he begged again, "what're we going to do now?"

"Nothing we can do, son. I played the only card I had that I thought might do some good. Money. As you saw, it didn't budge him. That Mr. Marcel sure sold him a bill of goods."

"You mean Gus and I have to leave because he wants to?"

"He's your pa. What he says goes. Looks like we got just one more day in more ways than one." The old man strode off into the darkness.

Eric could not sleep for thinking about leaving, and sometime during the night an idea came to him. He could hardly wait for morning to try it out.

Eric rose early, dressed quietly so as not to wake his father, tiptoed out the door, and hurried down the street into town. A few tourists wandered idly about the street and dock. The stores were just beginning to open. On a corner of the dock a pair of workmen were working on a frame that was beginning to take the shape of a stout cage. He turned in at

George Summer's store. From habit he hesitated and looked in the window at the display of wristwatches. He noted with a shock that the gold watch was gone. He had the strange feeling it was a bad omen.

The store was empty this early. George Summers was arranging cans of food on the shelves. He wiped his small hands on his apron and smiled at Eric. "You're out early, son. What can I do for you?"

Eric said, "I want to talk to you, Mr. Summers."

"Of course." George Summers came from behind the counter. "Fire away," he smiled.

Eric pointed out the door to where the two men were working on the cage. "Do you know what they're building?" He knew no other way to say it.

George Summers adjusted his gold-rimmed glasses and squinted through the door. "Beginning to look like some sort of cage."

"It is. It's to hold Gus."

"Your bear? You're not taking him away?"

"Pa is."

"What're you trying to tell me, Eric? That bear is important to this town. You know that."

"I know." Eric told him everything he knew about Henry D. Marcel and his son, what they had promised, and how Ten-Day Watson had tried to buy off his father. Eric finished with "I don't want to leave. Neither will Gus. I don't want him in a cage the rest of his life. Captain Nelson said he was important to the cruise business and I thought maybe you and some of the other people could talk to Pa. He might listen to you."

"We'll sure try. Oh, my! This is bad." George Summers removed his apron and laid it on the counter.

"Pa's asleep yet," Eric said. "You'd better give me about an hour to get him up." He started to leave, then added, "Pa'd be awful mad if he knew I'd told."

"He'll never know," George Summers said.

Eric hurried home. His father was not awake. Eric began making an extra amount of noise, lighting the fire and shoving pans and stove lids around. Soon his father rolled over and grumbled, "You have to make all that racket?"

"I'm getting breakfast," Eric said. "Do you want breakfast before I leave?" He kept clashing pans and stove lids.

Finally his father grumbled, "Might as well get up. Can't sleep with all this noise." He sat up, scratching his head and yawning, "How come you're makin' so much noise this morning?"

"I've got to get up to Mr. Watson's. This is the last day of the cruise ship for the year." He broke eggs into a pan and poured water into the coffeepot.

"That's no reason," his father muttered and headed for the washbasin.

They had just finished breakfast when George Summers and three of Tatouche's businessmen arrived. George Summers and Eddie Lang sat uncomfortably on the opposite side of the table from Ned Strong. Ted Benjamin and Bob Duncan sat on the unmade bed.

Eddie Lang was short and fat. If Ned Strong had a friend, other than the two old cronies he hung out with, Eddie Lang was it. Eddie said in his friendliest voice, "Ned, they're building a big cage on the dock this morning and we hear it's to take away Gloomy Gus."

Ned Strong glanced at Eric who was pretending to clean up the breakfast dishes at the little sink. "So, the kid's been talkin'."

George Summers said, "Do you think anybody could build that big and stout a cage in Tatouche without the word getting around?"

"All right," Eric's father agreed, "you hear right."

"Why, Ned?" Eddie Lang persisted. "You know how important that bear is to the town. If it hadn't been for him, Captain Nelson wouldn't have got interested in the first place. We'd still be dying on the vine. Now we've got a chance at a future. It's a little light after twenty years of darkness for Tatouche. Travel folders are telling about us. We're on the map. Money's coming into town with every plane, every cruise ship."

"That's right. We've got a chance to be a resort town," Bob Duncan added. "But if that bear leaves here, we'll lose a lot of our appeal to the tourists, according to this Captain Nelson."

Ned Strong calmly finished his coffee, enjoying the attention. He put the coffee cup down. "Seems like everybody makes big outa that bear, but me. And he's mine."

"I thought he was Eric's," Ted Benjamin said.

"My kid. So it's my bear."

"Joe Lucky says you get twenty-five cents for every tourist," Eddie Lang pointed out.

"That's what makes me mad," Ned Strong said. "You all say how much the bear's doin' for you and the town, and I get the least of all. I should be gettin' the most."

"You don't have to do a thing to collect that money," George Summers said.

"This Mr. Marcel is offerin' real money and I don't have to do anything."

The four men exchanged glances and Summers asked, "How much is he offering, Ned? Give us a chance to match it and keep the bear here."

"Mr. Marcel says they'll teach Gus tricks and things. In no time I'll get gettin' as much as five hundred a week for him. You come up with that and you've got a bear."

"Five hundred?" Ted Benjamin exploded. "You're crazy. You know we can't."

"Just a minute," Eddie Lang soothed. "Maybe we can. Five hundred a week for three months in the summer. If every business man in town chips in, maybe we can make it."

"Five hundred a week for the whole year," Ned Strong said.

Bob Duncan shook his head. "We can't when there's no cruise ships or planes in winter."

"Then, that's it," Ned Strong said.

"Maybe that bear's not yours to just take," Ted Benjamin said heatedly. "I understand he's Eric's bear. Maybe we'll just buy him from Eric."

"He's my kid, so he's my bear," Ned Strong repeated.

"Can't argue with that," George Summers agreed. "But don't you feel just a little bad going off and leaving us this way? As important as that bear is to the tourists, this whole thing that's just nicely got started could collapse."

"That's your problem. I'm lookin' out for number one."

"I thought I could talk to you, Ned," Eddie Lang said. "You and I have been pretty good friends for a long time. You know we can't pay that price. Aren't you at all interested in meeting us halfway?"

"I told you what you could have him for. That's it."

"Then we're wasting our time." Eddie Lang shook his head in defeat and shoved back his chair. "We might as well leave."

"Just a minute," Ted Benjamin said. "Eric ain't had his say. Eric, you want to leave here?"

Eric didn't dare look at his father. He shook his head and muttered, "No."

"Makes no difference," his father said. "Where I go, he goes. So's the bear."

"Why, you drunken bum..." Ted Benjamin began.

"Forget it, Ted," Eddie Lang said sharply. "Let's go."

After the men were gone Eric started to leave, and his father demanded, "Where do you think you're goin'?"

"There's tourists yet," Eric explained. "They'll want to see Gus."

"You come back as soon as they're gone. We've got to be ready to leave tomorrow morning. And keep that bear tied up tonight so we can go up early and get him and put him in the cage. And another thing — Joe Lucky'll be payin' you and Watson off tonight. You bring ours home. Don't try holdin' out on me."

"You always came for it," Eric reminded him.

"All right," his father said, "all right."

This day was like all the others, but it was different for Eric. He kept remembering that this would be the last time he'd be with Ten-Day Watson, Kenai, and Sitka. There'd be no more hikes across the soft, green tundra just to admire the country. He'd not see these great, clean mountains again, or lie on his back and stare up at the cloudless sky and listen to a silence so deep it was a pressure against his ears. He'd never watch Gus come padding across the tundra straight for him, looking for his handout of sweets. He'd never watch spring come with a rush that drove the snow back into the high hills as the North exploded in an orgy of growth. Tomorrow Gus and he would be heading south, away from this land he loved, and this spot that for the past three seasons had been more home than any other he had ever known. After today, Gus would be a caged bear, let out only to perform. His claws would be pulled and his big teeth torn out, leaving him a caricature of the great Alaskan Kodiak he once had been.

The day went all too fast and finally the last busload of tourists trooped down the trail talking and laughing. Eric and Ten-Day Watson took the sluice boxes from the creek and piled them against the cabin. The gold pans were scoured and stacked in the back room to await next year. They had finished when Joe Lucky returned.

He gave Watson half the money and the old man counted out Eric's share, forty dollars, and handed it to him. "Guess that's it for the year," Joe Lucky said. He strode over to Gus who was still chained to the tree, and stood looking at him. "If anybody had told me a bear could do what he did for a town, I wouldn't have believed it. The first thing people always asked was 'When do I see the bear?' That was all they talked about on the way back." He patted Gus's broad forehead. "Gonna miss you next year, big fella. Yes, sir, gonna miss you a lot." He shook hands with Eric. "Lots of luck down south." Then he went down the trail with long, swinging strides.

"You going to put Gus in the cage tonight?" Watson asked.

"Pa says leave him chained here." Eric scratched at the base of Gus's ears and the bear made rumbling sounds deep in his chest. "We'll be up early in the morning for him. I guess Pa's afraid somebody might turn him loose or something."

"I'll give him a big feed so he won't miss going hunting and digging around."

Eric tried to say something, but a solid lump in his stomach was pushing into his throat. He looked down and kept scratching Gus's ears. Gus lifted his big nose and sucked in a mighty breath of the boy. "I'll be up early to get him," Eric said and ran down the trail.

When he reached town, the cruise ship was a blaze of lights at the outer edge of the bay entering the open sea. A single fishing boat lay at the dock. The big cage was finished and Henry D. Marcel and Cliff were inspecting it. Cliff grinned at Eric. "This oughta hold him."

Mr. Marcel said sharply, "You didn't bring the bear?"

"He's chained to a tree. Pa didn't want to leave him in the cage all night. We'll go up early and get him."

"Just so we get him," Mr. Marcel said.

When Eric entered the cabin, his father asked immediately, "Did you bring the money?"

Eric handed him the forty dollars. He counted it and put it in his pocket. "All right. Let's get something to eat and go to bed. We've got to be up early."

Once again Eric could not sleep. He turned and tossed on his bunk, his mind dredging up one crazy scheme after another for staying here. The night passed and the schemes disappeared. They would leave just as his father had determined.

Eric was up early. He dressed quietly in the dark room and had just finished when his father's voice said, "It's too early to go after Gus."

"I couldn't sleep." He got into his jacket. "I'll go up and get Gus."

His father raised up in bed. The next minute he had lit the lamp and was staring hard at Eric. "Alone?"

"Gus knows me. I can lead him. If there's other people around, he might get excited or something and there'd be no holding him."

"All right," his father agreed. "I'll meet you at the cage. How long'll it take?"

64

"A couple of hours. Gus likes to poke along." He was turning toward the door when his father's voice stopped him.

"Don't get any cute ideas."

"What ideas, Pa?"

"You don't wanta leave. You've been tryin' to figure out somethin'."

"There's nothing to figure out."

"You remember that!" his father warned.

It was still dark, but the first faint glow of morning outlined the distant nest of mountain peaks. Eric hurried through the dark, quiet town, past the dock with its waiting cage and fishing boat, and went up the gravel road. He kept thinking of his father's warning. What could he try? Two hours from now they'd be on the small seiner heading out to sea to meet the freighter. He was halfway to Watson's when the answer rushed into his mind and stopped him. He was amazed at its simplicity. He wondered why he hadn't thought of it before. It began with, if they didn't get back in time they'd miss the freighter. If they missed the freighter they'd go nowhere. Then his mind locked on that one track, carried the thought further. Suppose he didn't go down with Gus at all?

The sun burst forth from behind the mountains flooding the earth with light and shining on the necklace of white mountain peaks. There was a huge, rugged land cut by countless valleys, canyons, and rivers, and a stand of timber that seemed to go on forever. A boy and a bear could become lost in there. He thought briefly of his father's anger, but that was not important. He'd take whatever punishment came to save Gus from life in a cage. He started running up the road.

Kenai came to meet him. He whispered, "Quiet, Kenai. Be quiet." Just possibly Ten-Day Watson was not yet awake. Or if he was, and Eric was quiet, he could get Gus away without the old man hearing. Sitka lay in front of the cabin. He turned his head, regarded Eric with big, liquid eyes, but did not get up.

Gus had wound his chain around the tree and was snuggled up close to the base lying with big head on forepaws. He rose and pushed his broad nose against Eric's hands searching for food. Eric found a single sugar cube in his pocket and gave it to him. He quietly unwound the chain from the tree and began leading Gus away. Then the cabin door opened and Ten-Day Watson came out. He looked at Eric and Gus and said, "I figured you might think of that."

"I don't want to leave here," Eric said. "I don't want Gus to spend the rest of his life in a cage."

"Neither do I," Watson said. "How're you going to do this?"

"We'll hide out in the hills. When we come back, the freighter will have gone and so will Henry D. Marcel."

Watson shook his head. "There's freighters passing along the coast every day or so. They can just stop another when they find you."

"They won't find us, and we'll stay out until they quit looking."

"They'll find you. Your pa won't quit — neither will the town. Sure, the whole town will turn out to look for you. Do you know why? When you don't show up at the dock this morning, they'll figure out Gus turned temporarily mean and did you harm, maybe even killed you. They'll be looking, not only for what's left of you, but for Gus — to kill him for a rogue Kodiak. They'll have half a dozen bush pilots out, and half a hundred men who know this country better than you do.

"But let's suppose you and Gus do manage to get away and they don't find you. You need a cabin and grub to live in that wilderness. There's no cabin for a hundred miles that I know of. And what're you going to eat? I'll give you a rifle and all the grub you can carry. But that won't last long. You can't live completely off the country by just eating meat. You need other things. I wouldn't dare bring grub out to you. Everybody knows how close you and me are. They'll figure I'm in on anything you do. Somebody'll be watching me all the time. But worst of all you won't have a cabin, and in a few weeks snow will be flying. Believe me, son, it'll never work."

Eric was silent a moment, an arm around Gus's big neck. "Then I'll take him far back in the hills and turn him loose," he said.

"It's not time for him to den up for the winter. He'll head right back here. He's been getting too well fed. Since he was a cub, he's associated this place with you and food."

"You turned loose a moose and a wolf that you'd raised from babies and made them go away. Why can't we do it with Gus?"

"That took months," Watson explained. "I had to make them wild again. When they came for food, I drove them away again and again until they finally knew there was none here for them. They went hungry more than once. Finally they never came back. There's no time to do that with Gus."

"What'll I do, Ten-Day?" Eric asked desperately. "What'll I do?"

"I've given that a lot of thought. I want you to listen to me real close. The day you found Gus on the tundra and brought him here you assumed all responsibility for him."

"He'd have died."

"That's not what I'm getting at. Listen to me. You raised Gus, fed him, and tamed him. You got him depending on you and liking you. You took the place of his mother that was killed. He looked to you for everything his mother would have given him — food, love, protection, and attention. And you gave it to him. Now he's your responsibility, no matter how big he is. You've got to keep faith with that responsibility. You can't hide Gus out and you can't drive him away. Some things can't be changed. They have to be faced and lived with. One way or another your pa is going to get Gus and you can't stop him; so don't make it hard on yourself and Gus by trying to avoid it. You've got to go with Gus and continue looking out for him. He'll be in a strange world and he's going to need a friend. You've got to go on being that friend. You can't shirk your responsibility to him now, when the going will be rough. That's when you have to stand fast more than ever."

"If we leave now we'll never come back." Eric choked.

"Never's a long time," Watson said gently.

"I thought you'd help us."

"If there was a way, you know I would. It's going to be lonesome here without you. We've had some mighty fine times. Nobody can take that away from us. If you ever need anything, if there's anything I can do, just write." He dug in his pocket and dangled the gold wristwatch that Eric had admired in George Summers' window for so long. "Picked it up on the way home the other night; thought you might like it."

Eric held the watch in his palm and turned it over. Watson had carefully scratched on the back of the case, "To Eric from T.D.W."

Watson strapped it on his wrist and said, "There, that looks fine. It was just made for you."

Eric tried to thank him, but no words came. He shook his head and looked away.

Watson squeezed the boy's arm and said, "On your way, son. They'll be looking for you and Gloomy Gus. Good luck. Good luck."

Eric walked down the trail with Gus lumbering along beside him. He wanted to look back just once more. But he didn't.

# PART II

❄

# Circus Days

# - 7 -

ERIC HAD NEVER been aboard a ship. He watched them lower Gus's cage into the dark hold and replace the hatch cover. He asked Mr. Marcel who was going to feed Gus, and the little circus man said, "The cook. You don't have to worry about it. It's all arranged."

A little later Eric went into the galley and found an older man and a young one busy peeling a mountain of potatoes. He guessed the older man was the head cook and asked, "Are you going to feed Gus?"

The man glanced at him and said, "If he eats, then I feed 'im. Who's Gus?"

"My bear."

"I thought he belonged to the little bald-headed guy."

"He's a circus man. He rents Gus. I raised him from a cub."

"No kidding? From a cub, eh?"

"Yes, sir. What are you going to feed him?"

"Well, I'll tell you. The fat guy said to give him table scraps. With twenty-five men on board that means lots of bread scraps, meat, some pastries, like hunks of pie, cake, doughnuts, and what's left over from some vegetables. That meet your approval?"

"Yes," Eric said. "Can I come when you feed him?"

"Why not? Harry here, feeds 'em. Once a day, the fat guy said. You be here right after supper tonight and he'll take you down with him."

That first night, Eric followed Harry down a series of ladders and through a maze of narrow compartments into Gus's dimly lit compartment. He sat on the steel deck before the cage and watched Gus eat. Afterward he scratched his stubby ears and talked to him for some time. Gus rumbled deep in his chest, shoved his big nose through the bars, and whoofed at Eric in greeting.

Life aboard ship was monotonous. Cliff spent all his time wandering among the crew talking with anyone who'd listen and showing pictures of himself as an animal trainer. Mr. Marcel always seemed busy with columns of figures. Ned Strong sat listlessly in a deck chair and stared out to sea, or walked aimlessly rubbing a hand over his mouth. He missed Eddie Lang's bar and his drinking cronies.

The third day, Eric was in the dim-lit compartment talking to Gus and scratching his ears when Cliff came. "I wondered where you disappeared to every day," he said.

Eric looked at him and said nothing.

"I don't want you hanging around Gus anymore," Cliff said. "I'm taking care of him now, understand?"

"You're not taking care of him," Eric said, "and Gus is lonesome. He needs me."

"Lonesome!" Cliff scoffed. "That big lug? Don't make me laugh. Go on, beat it. He's my responsibility now."

Eric rose. "I raised him. He's mine. I'm staying with him."

"You're getting out. He belongs to your old man and he's rented him to us. Besides, I'm the animal trainer, not you. That lets you out. Now get going."

"No!" Eric said.

Cliff's face was suddenly ugly. He moved forward, fists clenched. "I said get out. Now!"

"What goes on here?"

Neither boy had heard Henry Marcel come into the compartment. His black eyes darted from one to the other. "I've been wondering where both of you went. All right, let's have it."

"He keeps hanging around this bear," Cliff said, "and he's none of Eric's business now. I told him to keep away."

"Gus is lonesome and worried," Eric said. "He's never been in a cage before or down in a hole like this. He needs somebody he knows with him or he might get excited and tear this cage apart. Then there'd be plenty of trouble."

"Tear that cage apart?" Cliff laughed. "You're crazy."

"It's possible," Henry Marcel said thoughtfully. "That cage is wood. I'd hate to see him aroused and loose down here. It'd be a real job to cage him again. Eric knows the animal and you don't," he said to Cliff. "There's plenty of time for you to take over after we get to Seattle. Leave Eric alone and come on."

"But, Pa...," Cliff began.

"Come on!"

Cliff threw Eric an angry look, then followed his father.

So Eric spent his days in the dim-lit hold with Gus. Gus would lie pressed against the bars, big head on forepaws. Eric sat close, a hand reaching through from time to time to scratch an ear or tangle his fingers in the golden hair of the bear's neck or shoulder. He thought of Ten-Day Watson, Kenai and Sitka, and Friday Creek and listened to the endless throb of the propeller pushing them steadily farther away.

The seventh day they eased up to the dock in Seattle. The hatch cover was removed. Gus's cage was hoisted out and placed on the bed of a truck. The truck left the dock immediately and disappeared. A few minutes later Eric, his father, and the Marcels followed in a cab. They were whisked through the maze of concrete canyons of the city out into the suburbs.

Almost an hour later they stopped before the Henry D. Marcel and Son Continental Circus. Eric did not know what he expected the circus to look like, but not like this. It was composed of some twenty trucks of varying sizes, shapes, and colors and a number of four-wheeled trailers standing about in a school yard. A pair of elephants were staked to a chain near one truck and a knot of children were clustered about watching them eat. Six identical white horses were tied to the side of another truck. Directly before them four huge lions lounged in individual cages. In a truck near the lions, chimps screeched and rattled their cage doors.

Gus was already here. He had been transferred to a large cage that was fastened on a four-wheeled trailer. The trailer was hooked to the back of a truck.

Eric went to Gus, thrust his hands through the bars, and rubbed his ears and patted his head. Gus made grunting noises deep in his chest and pushed at Eric's hands searching for food. "It's all right, Gus," Eric said. "It's all right."

Behind him Cliff said, "Pa, when are we going to knock out those teeth and pull his claws so I can start working him?"

"Can't get a vet tonight. We'll do it first thing in the morning," Henry Marcel said. "You'd better change. People will start coming in very soon!"

Eric turned on Henry Marcel. "You're not really going to take out his teeth and claws."

"Of course. Your pa agrees."

"But he's not mean. You can see that."

"Can't depend on a bear. Cliff has to work him and that's what he wants."

"Pa," Eric turned to his father, "you're not going to let them do this to Gus."

Ned Strong shrugged. "He's just a bear."

"He's Gus, Pa."

"Makes no difference."

Before Eric could say more, the back door of a truck opened and a stocky, dark-haired man appeared. He came down the steps carefully one at a time, and Eric saw that one leg seemed to be shorter than the other. The man said, "Well, Henry, I see your trip was successful. That's the biggest bear I've ever seen." His voice was deep and pleasant.

"Very successful," Henry Marcel said. "Charlie Allen, Mr. Strong and his son, Eric. Mr. Strong owns the bear. Charlie runs things whenever I'm away. How's it been going?"

Charlie Allen shook hands with Eric and his father and

74

said, "Very good. We played to better than twelve thousand people the past three stops. We got here this morning and set up. We're ready to put on a show tonight."

"Then I'd better get a move on. Charlie, Mr. Strong and Eric will be staying with you as I wired you, so I'll leave them in your care." He hurried off toward a big white truck.

Charlie Allen said, "Bring your suitcases in and see where you're going to live. We've got four bunks in the truck and a cook stove. We cook our own meals and furnish our own grub in this circus. Your share will be fifteen dollars a week each, or thirty dollars for the two of you. We chip into the pot the beginning of each week. I'll do the cooking."

Ned Strong scowled. "Mr. Marcel didn't say nothin' about that."

"I guess he didn't think of it. It's standard practice in these small circuses that we take care of our own eating problems." Charlie Allen smiled. "We'll work out something. Come inside."

Eric's father rubbed a hand across his mouth and said, "You fellers go on in. I'll look around."

Eric watched the direction he took and remembered that several blocks back they'd passed a lighted tavern.

The inside of the truck held four bunks, two on each side, one above the other. There were hooks on the walls to hang clothing and a two-burner gas stove at the far end. The shelves above were full of food packages.

"This bunk's mine," Charlie Allen said. "You and your pa can have your pick of the other three. We'll shove your suitcases under this lower bunk."

"I'll take the upper one," Eric said. They shoved the suitcases under the bunk and Eric asked, "Does Mr. Marcel pay every week, Mr. Allen?"

"Every Saturday night. And Eric, the name's Charlie. We're going to be living pretty close in this truck so let's drop the formalities."

"All right. Then you'd better get your money for our food from Pa as soon as he's paid."

"I figured he had a problem. So he's gone looking for a drink."

"Yes."

"Too bad. I guess Henry Marcel didn't buy Gus as he'd planned. That why you're down here?"

"Pa wouldn't sell. Mr. Marcel is paying Pa a hundred dollars a week for the use of Gus."

"A hundred a week?"

"That's what Pa said."

"Pretty steep," Charlie observed dryly.

"Pa figures one of the really big shows will want Gus as soon as they hear about him," Eric said.

"Big shows! You mean what we used to call the Big Top, where they have hundreds of animals, huge tents, and five or six hundred people?"

"I guess so. Pa said Mr. Marcel told him that one of those big circuses might pay as much as four or five hundred dollars a week to use Gus, once they found out about him."

"Four or five hundred!" Charlie Allen shook his head amazed. "Are you sure your father was sober when he talked with Mr. Marcel?"

"He was when I got home and Mr. Marcel hadn't been gone too long."

"Does your father have some sort of contract with Mr. Marcel guaranteeing him that hundred a week?"

"I don't know. Is there something wrong?"

"Let's say there's something odd. Maybe I shouldn't be talking to you about this, but you and your pa are obviously complete strangers to circus life, so I'm going to tell you a few things you should know. You'll discover them soon anyway. First, there are no Big Tops, no big shows left."

"But Mr. Marcel said…"

"There are only a couple of Big Tops in business anymore, Eric. The chances of them being interested in Gus are mighty slim. There's a lot of little circuses like this one touring the country. If you'd lived in the south forty-eight, you and your pa would probably know that. A hundred dollars a week

76

for the use of an untrained bear is a terrific price."

"But Gus is the only tame Kodiak in the world," Eric pointed out.

"Which makes him worth more, naturally," Charlie agreed. "But a small circus like this can't afford to put out that kind of money. I don't know what Henry Marcel has in mind," he said thoughtfully. "He's a sharp operator."

"Should I tell Pa?"

Charlie considered, biting his lip. "I've a feeling he wouldn't believe us. I don't see anything to be gained by kicking up a fuss now. It's really none of your business or mine. Your pa should have a contract. Since he is here, he might as well go on collecting his money as long as he can."

"Does Mr. Marcel own all these trucks and animals and things?"

"Only the truck Cliff and he drive and live in, and the two black bears Cliff works. These other acts and the equipment that goes with them belong to the people who perform the acts. Henry Marcel is a promoter, a man with money who organized this circus. He signed up the different acts. He put the show together. For a man with no previous circus experience he's done a good job."

"Do you have an act?"

"Not with this broken hip. My brother and I had a high-wire act in one of the Big Tops years ago. The Allen Brothers. We were good," he smiled thoughtfully. "One night Paul slipped, as near as we could ever figure. He fell against me and we both went down. He was killed and I was left like this. There's no place on a high wire for a man with a short leg. But circus is all I know. I was born on the road between two cities somewhere in the Midwest."

"What do you do now?"

"I guess you'd call me an assistant to the promoter. There's not much about circuses I don't know. I handle things when Henry Marcel is away and offer advice now and then. For that I have the concessions — candy, pop, hot dogs, snow cones, and novelties." He glanced at his watch. "We've got a little time before the show. Let's take a walk. I'll introduce you around."

The sun was gone. Dusk had settled in. A cool breeze blew across the school yard from the distant sea. The first people had straggled in and were walking about. The crowd of children around the elephants had grown.

"A circus is a tight-knit organization," Charlie explained. "You'll find these fine people." They passed the lion cages. The big cats lay staring balefully out between the bars. "Give them a wide berth," Charlie cautioned. "A couple of these cats wait until somebody comes close, then they reach out and grab." He called into the open door of a truck, "Hey, Chet."

A young, handsome blond man came out wearing a white shirt, tight white pants, and knee-high shiny black boots. A pistol was strapped around his middle.

"Eric, this is Chet Olds. You'll see him put the lions through their paces tonight. Eric and his father own the big Kodiak that came in today."

Olds smiled and shook hands. "That bear of yours must be two or three times as big as one of my cats."

"The lions look a lot fiercer," Eric said.

"They're fierce enough."

"How's the hand?" Charlie asked. "One of the cats got a claw into him a couple of weeks ago," he said to Eric.

Olds held out his right hand and Eric saw the scars as big as a nickel on the back. "Claw didn't go quite all the way through," he explained, wiggling his fingers. "Another week and it'll be as good as new."

One of the lions let out an angry roar that made Eric jump. Chet Olds said, "See you later, Eric. Glad you're with us." He went toward the cages.

"Did he ever have to shoot a lion with that pistol?" Eric asked.

"That's just for looks. If it's loaded, they're blanks."

Eric met the Marletto Brothers, Ed and Bobby, who were dressing in their truck for their trampoline act. Then Ken Tucker, who did the slide-for-life and performed on the tight wire with his wife, Clara. "We got a boy your age," Clara smiled. "We'd like to make a lawyer out of him if we can keep him away from the circus lot."

Mario, who worked the elephants, Rose and Jennie, was a huge, black-browed, big-chested man. "Eric," he smiled, "it's good to have a boy around. Come see me anytime. But leave that bear of yours at home."

There were Franz and Joso, the tumblers; Joe and Rusty, the clowns, who were already dressed in their outlandish costumes and were clumping about in snowshoe-sized shoes. Edna, a small, neat woman in a silver costume, was tying plumes in the manes of her six performing liberty horses. Billy Markson's four chimps were the noisiest of all. They rattled their cages and screamed at Eric. "Just showing off," Billy explained.

"Chimps are the smartest animals of all," Charlie said as they walked away, "and the meanest, too."

They visited every truck and act that made up the circus. Eric lost track of their names and the acts they performed.

The street lights came on. In the distance the city's core threw a high fan of light into the night sky. Light gushed out the open doors of the gymnasium. Music blasted into the quiet evening. Long strings of cars began arriving on every street. They parked bumper to bumper along the curbs, filled vacant lots and driveways. People began moving toward the gymnasium from every direction. Adults walked swiftly, the kids dashed ahead shouting and laughing.

Charlie said, "Here they come. Looks like it'll be a good crowd when they start coming this thick. I've got to go to work."

They followed the crowd to the gymnasium. Just outside the big doors, Eric found the popcorn machine, candy-floss machine, and a counter piled high with snow cones, a mixture of crushed ice and syrup in a cone-shaped paper cup. There was a hot-dog stand, candy counter, and balloon novelties. Men in white jackets and caps, with trays slung around their necks, were loading up and disappearing inside.

"Concessions," Charlie explained. "We call them joints. The peddlers with the trays and white jackets are called butchers." Charlie slipped into a white coat and cap and handed Eric a bag of popcorn. "Go inside and see the show. You're part of this outfit now."

The gymnasium was brilliantly lighted. The seats, rising tier on tier along the walls, were filling with people. Two huge performing cages had been set up in the center of the floor. Chairs, bars, mats, a springboard, the high wire, and slide-for-life were in place. Music came from an electronic organ and amplifying system A single drummer accompanied the organist.

Eric found a seat on the top row and settled down to watch his first circus.

Henry Marcel, dressed in a black suit, white shirt, and black bow tie, was master of ceremonies. He whistled in each act and introduced it over the P.A. system. Each trick was accompanied by booming organ music, the rattle of the snare drum, the thump of the bass, and Mr. Marcel's remarks, "The greatest! death-defying! internationally famous! only act of its kind in the entire world!"

For two hours Eric sat gripped in the magic of wild animals and people performing unbelievable feats. Cliff Marcel and his two black bears came on near the end. Cliff got the big-music-and-drums buildup and his father's shouted announcement, "The world's youngest trainer of wild animals, Cliff Marcel, with his brawny bruins." Cliff trotted in, dressed in a glittering, tight-fitting gold uniform, his black hair slicked down, carrying a long whip and leading two good-sized, muzzled black bears. Even from where he sat Eric could see that their claws had been pulled. Cliff cracked his whip and put the bears through their acts. They rode bicycles, balanced on rubber balls, did a teeter-totter act, sat on stools and lifted their paws in a hands-up gesture. Finally they stood on their hind legs at either side of Cliff while he took his bow.

The lion act wound up the show. Eric stood ready to leave when Henry Marcel shouted into the mike, "Ladies and

Gentlemen," The Henry D. Marcel and Son Continental Circus always aims to give you your money's worth. We have presented the finest, most thrilling acts that can be found. In keeping with that tradition, the Henry D. Marcel and Son Continental Circus wishes to give you the rare privilege of the first peep at our latest acquisition, which arrived just this afternoon and will be trained and exhibited by Cliff Marcel, the world's youngest animal trainer. Ladies and Gentlemen, from the wilds of Alaska, we present the biggest carnivorous animal on earth, the only tame Kodiak bear in the world, Gloomy Gus!" Henry Marcel pointed dramatically to the big double doors. The organ crashed, the snare drum rolled, and the bass boomed.

Five men pushed and pulled a huge four-wheeled cage into the gymnasium with Gus inside. Cliff marched ahead, arms raised, smiling, bowing.

Gus's big nose was thrust between the bars. His stubby ears were erect as he blinked curiously at the mass of people. Eric could see his nose wrinkle as he sucked in the aroma of cigars, cigarettes, candy, hot dogs, popcorn, and a hundred other scents too delicate for any human nose to catalogue.

The organ and drums stopped. The crowd was held silent in wonder at Gus's size. The two blacks that Cliff had performed with earlier had been large bears, but compared to Gus, they seemed small. The men pulled the cage slowly around the room and out the doors again. Henry Marcel said, "Ladies and Gentlemen, the only tame Kodiak bear in the world, straight from Alaska, Gloomy Gus; and the Henry D. Marcel and Son Circus has him!"

The organ burst into the exit march. The show was over.

Eric made his way back to the truck. The crowd scattered across the dark school yard to their cars talking and laughing. In minutes the streets were empty again. The organ music stopped. The lights went out in the gymnasium.

Gus's cage had been returned to the truck, and his black bulk was pressed against the bars. Eric thrust both hands through and scratched his ears and patted his broad forehead.

"You sure surprised everybody," he said. "How did it feel to have a thousand people looking at you?" Gus sniffed at his hands and rumbled deep in his chest. "I guess you feel lonesome," Eric said. "Me, too. I wish we were back at Ten-Day Watson's."

Charlie Allen limped out of the night and handed Eric a ball of pink cotton candy. "Thought your friend might like this."

Eric pulled off chunks and held them in his palm. Gus lifted the bits deftly, smacking his lips. When it was gone, he gave Gus a couple of pats on the head and followed Charlie into the truck. Charlie flopped on his bunk with a sigh, leaned back against the wall, and closed his eyes. Suddenly he looked twenty years older and very tired. "How did you like your first circus?" he asked without opening his eyes.

Eric sat down on the bunk across the narrow aisle. "It was exciting. I didn't know animals could learn so many tricks. And those things the people, the performers, did — balancing and all."

"Practice. Hours, days, weeks and weeks, sometimes years of practice."

"He said Gus was the biggest Kodiak in the world. We don't know that for sure."

Charlie smiled, "That's something you have to understand about circuses, Eric. People come to be thrilled, excited, amazed, maybe frightened a little; but above all, entertained for a couple of hours. Entertainment is a circus's only reason for being. The M.C.'s spiel plays a big part in it. Sure, some may guess that Gloomy Gus isn't the biggest Kodiak on earth, that the Marletto Brothers aren't Europe's greatest trampoline artists, that Chet Olds isn't the world's foremost lion tamer, but it's all part of the buildup for the act. It helps make entertainment and you saw how they loved it. We try to give them their money's worth. You said it was exciting. The M.C. helped make it so."

"Well," Eric smiled, "it was exciting."

"Then it was a successful performance." Charlie began

rubbing his hip. "It aches when I've been on my feet too long."

"How long has it been?"

"All day yesterday, last night, and today."

"Without sleep?"

Charlie nodded. "We put on a show last night in Portland. After the show we knocked down, packed, and drove all night to get here. It took most of the day to get ready for this show. Sleep is something you get when there's nothing important to do."

"How long will we be here?"

"We're through. A couple of the acts will head across the city for our next stop tonight. Most of us will spend the night here because we need the rest, knock down early, drive over tomorrow, and rush to set up for the night's performance."

"It sounds like hard work," Eric said.

"Never let the customer know that. You appear bright-eyed and full of pep if it kills you." Charlie began unbuttoning his shirt. "Tell me about Gloomy Gus and the North. I've always wanted to see it."

Eric leaned against the wall of the truck, pulled up his legs, and began to talk while Charlie undressed. His gray eyes were dreamy and a faint smile played about his lips. Once again, he sat on a barren knoll and heard a tiny cub trying to nurse its dead mother. He was back in Tatouche with Ten-Day Watson, Kenai, and Sitka. He saw the ring of snowcapped mountains and felt the vast silence. He saw the birds return in the spring and the ice go out of Friday Creek. He saw the cruise ships sail into the bay and the tourists troop up to see Gus and to pan gold. When he finished, Charlie lay on his bunk, hands folded behind his head.

"Sounds like a wonderful country," Charlie said. "No wonder you love it. Then Gloomy Gus really belongs to you and not your pa." He glanced at his watch. "It's close to midnight. How soon do you figure he'll be in?"

"There's no telling. We were seven days on that boat."

"And he worked up quite a thirst."

"Yes."

Charlie shook his head. "The three of you would have been better off if you'd stayed in Tatouche. You had a good thing going with the tourists coming in."

"Gus would have been better off," Eric said bitterly as the thought of tomorrow morning came rushing back. "They're going to knock out his big teeth and pull his claws."

"Whose idea is that?"

"Cliff's. He keeps telling it to his father. I don't want it done." Eric's smoldering resentment at Cliff Marcel boiled out. "I handled Gus all the time and I never had any trouble. Why should he? He's an animal trainer."

"He's no trainer."

"What do you mean? I watched him tonight."

"He's a show-off. He just puts those bears through the tricks a real animal trainer taught them. There's a number of fellows like Cliff around. They think that dressing up in a fancy suit, making an animal perform, and popping a whip and taking bows is going to make them rich or famous. He wants to pull Gus's teeth and claws because he's afraid of him. Cliff hasn't the faintest idea how to handle him or begin training him. It would take months for a good trainer to do anything with Gus at his age. Henry Marcel can't afford that time. He has to show Gus now and start getting some of his money back, so Cliff has to do the best he can."

"If they pull his teeth and claws, he won't be the same Gus. I saw those bears of Cliff's tonight and I could see from up in the top row that their claws were pulled. It ruined the bears for me. You said Mr. Marcel listens to you. Can't you stop him?"

Charlie shook his head. "This concerns his son and I've learned that most anything Cliff wants he gets. What does your pa say?"

"He doesn't care as long as he gets paid."

"Then that's it. He's the only one who has the authority to stop them. If it will be any comfort to you, a good vet can do the job and Gus will know very little pain."

"It'll ruin him," Eric insisted, "just like those black bears are ruined."

"Another thing," Charlie went on, "actually Gus won't miss those claws and teeth. He's a circus bear now. He'll never need to dig or tear anything again."

"They're part of him," Eric insisted. "He's supposed to be big and fierce, from the wilds of Alaska. Then they're going to bring him out for people to see muzzled and with his claws and teeth gone. Alaskans would laugh at him."

"I know how you feel." Charlie slid down under the single blanket. "But that's how it is. We can't change it. I'm sorry. Now I've got to get some sleep. Big day ahead. You'd better turn in, too. You can douse the light."

Eric climbed into the upper bunk, undressed, turned out the light, and slid under the blanket. It was hot and stuffy. There was no ventilation in the truck. He thought of Gus and tomorrow morning and the show he'd seen and the people he'd met. Voices shouted somewhere. Tires howled, a horn blared. A truck motor started up in the school yard, then another and another. He listened as they rumbled out onto the street. Part of the circus was already moving on to the next stop. A lion coughed and another answered. In the truck next to them a chimp rattled the door of his cage and began screeching. Then they were all at it. Billy Markson's angry voice quieted them down. This would be his and Gus's life from now on. A great longing tightened his throat and he turned his face to the wall.

Much later Eric heard his father stumble up the steps, enter the truck, and flop on the bunk with a noisy sigh. He had left the door open and thin light from a distant streetlight entered the truck. Eric crawled down, removed his father's shoes, loosened his belt and shirt, and pulled a blanket over him. The smell of liquor was very strong. He stood a moment looking down at the slack face. With his father nothing had changed.

# - 8 -

NED STRONG was still asleep the next morning and Eric and Charlie had just finished breakfast when a pickup pulled in beside their truck. Through the open door Eric saw the black letters on the side. Dr. H. E. French, Veterinarian. Eric went out immediately followed by Charlie. The young veterinarian was talking with Cliff and Henry Marcel. "You have a bear here you want declawed and some teeth removed?"

"That's right." Henry Marcel nodded at Gus. "Him!"

The veterinarian stepped close to the cage and looked at Gus. Gus stood, big nose poked through the bars, and looked back at the young man. "I thought you meant one of those small black bears. What in the world is this thing, a grizzly?"

"A Kodiak," Henry Marcel said. "The only tame one in the world."

"What's the difference?" Cliff Marcel demanded. "A black or a Kodiak. You can do it, can't you? You're supposed to be a vet."

"I can do it," the vet said in an annoyed voice. "But it's harder with an animal this size."

"Then let's get at it," Henry Marcel said. "We've got to move across town to another location and be ready for a show this evening."

The vet opened his bag on the tailgate of the pickup and began selecting instruments. "Somebody hold his attention so I can give him a shot and put him to sleep."

Cliff Marcel pointed at Eric. "He'll do that."

Eric looked at Cliff, then at Henry Marcel. "I won't."

Henry Marcel said angrily, "We've got no time to fool around, boy. Get up here and keep this animal quiet so the vet can shoot him."

"No." Eric looked at Charlie and began backing away. Charlie was rubbing his jaw thoughtfully and watching Henry Marcel.

"Where's your pa?" Henry Marcel demanded. "Where's Ned Strong? He'll make you do it."

"Pa's asleep," Eric said.

"Asleep or drunk?" Marcel demanded angrily.

"Henry, you could be making a big mistake," Charlie said quietly.

"So I'm making a mistake," Marcel said. "Let's get on with it."

The veterinarian moved up to the cage holding the hypodermic needle. "If someone will get the animal's attention…"

"It could cost you an awful lot of money," Charlie said to Marcel, "but then, that's your business."

"Cost me money? How do you figure?"

"…Somebody talk to the bear or show him something to eat," the veterinarian said. "I'll only take a second or two."

"Hold it," Henry Marcel said. "What do you mean, Charlie, this will cost me a lot of money?"

Eric held his breath and watched Charlie Allen. The short, stocky man, he felt, was fighting for Gus. Charlie leaned against the side of the trailer and said calmly, "I don't know what it cost you to get this animal down here. But being the only tame Kodiak in the world, I do know you've got quite an attraction. Naturally, you'll do a lot of advertising and that's expensive. People will flock to see this bear because you've come up with two magic names, Kodiak and Alaska."

"What're you driving at?" Marcel asked, annoyed.

"You don't have to teach him a lot of tricks. If you do, you've got just another performing bear. People won't associate him with the wilds of Alaska and the biggest bear on earth. They'll associate him with any other bear that rides a bicycle or balances on a ball. That's not what you're going to advertise if you're smart, and it's not what you want."

"What's that got to do with taking out his teeth and claws?" Cliff Marcel demanded.

"Just this. In a big show, under canvas, the audience is sitting far enough away so they can't see fine details. Here, with us holding shows in school gymnasiums and fairground buildings, the audience is so close they can see an animal's eyelashes. Take a good look at Gloomy Gus. He looks big and fierce, doesn't he? He looks like the biggest bear on earth from the wilds of Alaska. Now pull those big teeth and take out his claws and put a muzzle on him. Everybody will be able to see that. You think he's going to look fierce then? Ask the doctor?"

"Well," Dr. French smiled, "he'd still be big."

"You'll make a laughing stock of the very thing you're trying to promote," Charlie said. "Your advertising will backfire on you. After a few times people won't be coming to see him. He'll lose his drawing appeal because he'll be just another toothless, clawless, muzzled bear."

"You've got to take those teeth and claws out," Cliff Marcel insisted. "You can't handle a bear with teeth and claws."

"The good trainers do it all the time," Charlie said quietly. "They want the audience to realize the chances they're taking. That's part of the thrill of the act."

"You're an old circus man," Henry Marcel said. "What do you suggest?"

"Don't try to teach him any tricks. I don't think you can anyway. He's too old. Just lead him out there and let people see how big he is. If he'll stand on his hind legs to show off his height, or do any other little trick, fine. If not, forget it. Just to look at him close up is all that's really necessary."

"You think people will come just to see a bear walk around?" Cliff demanded.

"They will for this one. You've never heard of a trained gorilla, but Ringling featured one for years. They kept him in a glassed-in, air-conditioned cage, and people came by thousands to see him. They'll do the same with Gloomy Gus, because he happens to be the only tame Kodiak in the world."

Henry Marcel nodded thoughtfully. "I never thought of that angle. I have got a lot invested in this animal. You figure showing him is all that's really necessary?"

"Absolutely. People will come to see him because of what he is, not to see him perform. If he happened to do a couple of simple little tricks, that's fine. But Kodiaks don't lend themselves to training. I know a man who tried it. The bear ended up in a zoo."

"Pa, we agreed to this," Cliff said. "Charlie's siding with Eric because Eric don't want his old bear touched. What's Charlie know about this? He's a crippled-up high-wire man. He's no trainer."

Henry Marcel shook his head. "Charlie was raised circus. What he says makes sense. I can't take any chances losing my investment."

"So a few people sitting close will notice his claws and teeth are gone. It won't matter."

"It'll matter. Forget trying to train him. We're going to show him off, that's all." He turned to Dr. French. "I've changed my mind."

Dr. French nodded and began putting instruments back in his bag. "You owe me seven-fifty for the trip."

"You didn't do anything."

"I took the time from my office to make this call."

"I'll pay when you do something," Henry Marcel said.

Dr. French started to argue, thought better of it, and got in his pickup and drove off.

"All right, let's get moving," Marcel said. "When we get settled this afternoon, you take Gus out and lead him around, get acquainted with him."

"How about a muzzle, Pa? He can at least have a muzzle."

"No muzzle. Eric never used one. If he can do it, you can. You want to be an animal trainer. Well, here's your chance."

A few minutes later pickups, campers, and trailers with their various cages attached began pulling out of the schoolyard.

Eric, in the cab of the second truck with Charlie, smiled and said, "You saved Gus. Thanks."

"Like I told you last night. Henry Marcel hasn't had too much circus experience, so if I approach him the right way and if my timing is good, he'll usually listen to me. Apparently the approach and the timing were so perfect even Cliff couldn't ruin it."

Eric smiled. "It's going to surprise Pa when he wakes up."

"When do you figure that'll be?"

"It depends on when he gets in. Last night it was just after midnight, so it might be around noon."

"He does this often?"

"Whenever he has money."

"And he'll be getting some every week now. Guess you haven't had an easy life."

"I spent most of my time at Ten-Day Watson's with Gus." Eric said in a rush, "I know Pa owes you money for grub for both of us. Maybe Mr. Marcel would give it to you out of what he pays Pa."

"Don't let it worry you," Charlie smiled. "We'll figure out something."

The new location was a roller-skating rink. It was a huge wooden building that covered an entire block. They parked among the trees at the side of the building and everyone began pulling equipment out of trucks, carrying it inside to set up. Eric helped Charlie with the popcorn and cotton-candy machines. When they finally returned to the truck, Eric's father was standing outside looking through the bars at Gus.

"When they gonna pull his claws an' teeth?" he asked.

"They decided not to," Eric said.

"Why?"

"They figured it wasn't necessary."

"Hm-m-m. You workin?" he asked Eric.

"I'm helping Charlie."

"You gettin' paid for it?"

"Everybody pitches in and helps set up for a performance," Charlie said.

"Not everybody." Ned Strong went off down the street.

Once they had everything in the building, the Marletto Brothers, Ed and Bobby, unfastened Gus's trailer from the camper. Mario brought Rose over. The elephant put her broad forehead against the end of the trailer and with the Marletto Brothers steering pushed the trailer up against the open door of the building.

Cliff appeared in his gold costume, carrying his whip and a short length of chain. He looked at Gus and swallowed nervously.

"All right," Henry Marcel said, "take him out and walk him around the building so he gets used to you and being in a big room. Don't try to get him to do tricks. You got a pocketful of hard candy?"

Cliff nodded, not taking his eyes from Gus. "No reason we can't muzzle him."

"We've got no muzzle that will fit," Henry Marcel said. "Get the chain on him, lead him into the building, and walk him around. Go on."

Cliff suddenly shoved the chain into Eric's hands. "He knows you. Put it on him."

Ed Marletto winked at Eric, unsnapped the padlock, and opened the cage door.

Eric thrust his hand in and said, "Come on, Gus. Come on out. I'll bet you're tired of that old cage." Gus thrust his big head through the door, lifted his black nose, and whoofed mightily at Eric. He began pushing at his hands looking for food. Eric said, "Nothing doing. Not yet." He patted Gus's broad forehead and scratched at the base of his stubby ears. Gus rumbled deep in his chest. Eric snapped the chain around his neck and started to lead him out when Cliff shouldered him roughly aside.

"All right, give me the chain. Come on, give it to me." He snatched the chain from Eric's hands. "Come on, Gus. Come on." He tugged on the chain. When Gus was in no hurry, he held out a piece of hard candy. Gus lifted it deftly from his palm and ambled through the door. "Everybody back," Cliff said. "Get outa the way." He pulled on the chain and held out another piece of candy. Gus took it and followed him through the door smacking his lips.

Henry Marcel said, "Charlie, go in with him and see how he makes out."

Cliff called, "I know what I'm doing. I don't need any help." He offered Gus another piece of candy.

Charlie went in and Eric started to follow. Cliff said sharply, "You stay out. If you come in, Gus'll be looking for you and I won't be able to do a thing with him. From now on you keep away, clear away. I want him to forget you. Don't feed him anymore and don't go near his cage."

Eric was about to answer angrily when Charlie squeezed his arm. "I won't be long. Why don't you wait in the truck for me?"

Fuming with anger, Eric returned to the truck and sat on Charlie's bunk. From time to time the muffled sounds of voices came through the walls of the building. Once he heard Cliff's voice say angrily, "Come on, Gus. Come on. Don't be so stupid."

An hour later Charlie returned. He sat on the bunk beside Eric and sighed.

"How did it go?" Eric asked.

"All I did was sit there. Nobody can tell Cliff anything. He knows it all. He thinks you're not handling an animal unless you're forcing him to do some trick. It takes all the patience in the world to make a good trainer. And Cliff doesn't have that."

"He didn't hit Gus with that whip?" Eric asked.

Charlie smiled. "He knows better. It would be unwise and very dangerous. He just carried the whip for looks and effect. Someplace he saw a picture of a lion tamer who carried a blacksnake. So he does it. He pops it and points and threatens with it, but he's not so foolish as to hit an animal with it. He just led Gus around the room and fed him pieces of hard candy. He did try to get Gus to stand up and to sit on a stool, but Gus didn't know what he wanted and Cliff doesn't know how to show him."

"I've got to see Gus," Eric started up. "That Cliff can't tell me to stay away from him."

Charlie caught his arm and pulled him back on the bunk. "Sit still and listen to me."

Eric grumbled, "That stupid Cliff in his gold suit. Who does he think he is?"

"I agree," Charlie said, "but this time he happens to be right. You've got to stay away from Gus. You've got to stop feeding him and making over him. Cliff's handling him now, not you. They've got to know each other."

"He says he wants Gus to forget me," Eric said angrily. "Well, Gus won't. I raised Gus from a cub."

"Of course, he won't forget you," Charlie agreed. "But if you stay away and Cliff keeps working with him and feeding him, Gus's memory will become a little dim. Gus has got to become dependent on Cliff now, not you."

"But Gus is mine. I didn't agree to keep away from him when we came down here."

"You've got to now, for Gus's good and the act he has to put on. You'd better face it, both Gus and you belong to your father, and he's rented Gus to this circus with the understanding that Cliff Marcel is to handle him. If Cliff says stay away, so his job can be made easier, than that's what you do."

"But Gus is alone down here. He needs a friend, someone that knows him and understands him."

"Gus will be all right. He'll adjust to circus life without much trouble if you leave him alone. So don't make it harder for him. If you love Gus, keep away from him, so he can make this adjustment."

"But who'll look after him and care for him?"

"Cliff will feed him and care for him. If it'll make you feel better, I'll look in on Gus every day and make sure that he's being well treated."

"All right," Eric agreed finally. "But I don't like it."

"Neither do I," Charlie said. "But don't blame Cliff or Henry Marcel. Cliff's just trying to do a job he's not equipped for, and Henry is trying to get some money back on his investment."

Within half an hour Gus's trailer was moved down to the last truck in the line, as far from Eric as possible. The last Eric saw of him was his big nose stuck between the bars as Rose shoved the cage along.

That night after the show they left the city and headed out into the country, traveling from town to town, putting on a show in each one, then driving half the night to reach the next. Eric liked the small towns. The people were more friendly than in the cold, impersonal city.

Eric caught only occasional glimpses of Gus these days. He missed sitting by Gus's cage and scratching his ears and listening to him rumble deep in his chest. And he missed the soft brush of the bear's lips on his palm as he daintily lifted some tidbit of food.

Charlie reported that Cliff was taking good care of Gus. "I visit him every day, too. Gus and I have become friends. I think Cliff will show him soon. He can't stall much longer. His father's getting impatient."

"What's he waiting for?"

"He's afraid Gus might start acting up in front of a crowd. He feels that if he knows him better he'll be able to handle him if he does."

"Gus won't act up. He paid no attention to crowds in Tatouche."

"I know. Cliff's afraid of Gus because he still has his teeth and claws and isn't muzzled. What he doesn't know and may never learn is that you can't handle an animal you fear."

From town to town the performance never varied. They played in school gyms, lodge halls, fairground exhibit halls, anywhere the building was large enough and the door high enough to get Jennie and Rose through. Eric soon tired of watching the performance and took to wandering the streets while the show was in progress. Several times he found his father in a bar and got him back to the truck into his bunk before the show ended and it was time to knock down for the next move. Once Charlie and he had to stay behind to hunt for Ned Strong. The rest of the circus went on to the next town. Thereafter Eric made a special effort to keep track of his father. But Ned Strong made no effort to pay Charlie for their share of the food and this continued to worry Eric.

Charlie finally suggested, "How'd you like to be a butcher? We could put a white jacket and cap on you and you could sell pop and candy through the crowd during the show. Whatever you made would help pay yours and your pa's grub bill."

"You think I could do it?"

"There's nothing to it. Just be sure you always pour the pop into a paper cup. Don't give anybody a bottle. He might get excited and throw it."

"All right," Eric agreed.

That was the night Cliff Marcel decided to show off Gus for the first time.

# - 9 -

ERIC WANDERED through the crowd dressed in his white jacket and cap, a tray slung from a strap around his neck. The tray was loaded with bottles of pop, candy, and paper cups. He was surprised how much he sold. By intermission he had refilled the tray twice.

Edna and her liberty horses opened the second half of the show. She was followed by Franz and Joso, the tumblers. The Marletto Brothers' trampoline act drew a good hand. Eric emptied his tray and went out for a refill. When he returned, Mario was putting Jennie and Rose through their paces. Joe and Rusty did a three-minute comedy routine while the roustabouts got the heavy elephant props out of the way. Then Cliff and his two black bears came on. Eric heard the popping of Cliff's whip above the drum and organ music, but he didn't look up. He'd seen enough of Cliff's strutting as he played animal trainer. Finally he heard the exit music and knew Cliff and the bears were going out the big doors at the end of the hall. There was mild applause.

Chet Olds' lion act followed the black bears and that would be the end of the show.

Eric started working toward the end of the hall so he could get out ahead of the crowd. Halfway down the hall he was held up when he sold four candy bars and a bottle of pop and had to make change for a five-dollar bill. A boy in the front row signaled for a bottle of pop. The lion act ended with a good hand for Chet Olds. Eric opened the bottle of pop, thinking that the exit march was about to begin and this would be his last sale. Then Mr. Marcel's voice blared over the P.A. system:

"And now, Ladies and Gentlemen, a special treat. For the first time in any circus, from the wilds of the great North, Alaska, the Henry D. Marcel and Son Continental Circus brings you the greatest carnivorous animal on earth, the world's largest bear. The only tame Kodiak in the world — the one and only Gloomy Gus!"

Eric forgot the boy who was holding out his hand for the drink, forgot the open bottle of pop he held. He stood transfixed, almost in the act of pouring into the paper cup. His eyes were riveted on the far doors. Organ music blasted through the room. The snare drum let go with a roll that went on and on. The base thundered. With a crash of cymbals all sound stopped. Through the far door padded Gus with his pigeon-toed stride. A surprised murmur rippled through the room. Then silence. A thousand pairs of eyes centered on the huge bear. A spotlight trapped him in its glare. Muscles bunched and rippled. His loose-fitting golden hide glistened.

Cliff Marcel strode beside him in his tight-fitting suit holding the end of a chain snapped about Gus's neck. He popped his whip with a flourish and raised his arm and smiled. He gave Gus a piece of candy. The bear chomped it, smacking his lips and looking about unconcerned, as he paced along beside Cliff. The organ music burst forth again.

They had covered half the length of the room when Gus lifted his head and his small eyes spotted Eric with the pop bottle in his hand. Gus broke into a trot, licking his lips, eyes fixed on the bottle.

Cliff hauled back on the chain and cracked his whip, but Gus paid no attention. Cliff was forced to trot to keep abreast of Gus. He yanked on the chain again and started to crack the whip. His toe caught under the edge of a mat that had been left by a previous act. He tripped and went flat. He had wrapped the chain around his hand and could not let go. He was dragged headfirst into a second mat. The mat bunched against his head and shoulders. They struck a springboard, upended it, and dragged it along. A chair, a pedestal, went flying. Gus skirted the trampoline, dragging Cliff, the springboard, and the mat into it. The trampoline tipped over on top of Cliff. Cliff began screaming at Gus, but his voice was lost in the blaring of the organ, the rolling of the snare drum. Gus's little pig eyes were fixed on Eric and the bottle in his hands.

Too late, Eric realized why this was happening and started to back hurriedly away. Gus was upon him. He threw up his big head and his black nose struck the bottom of the tray. Candy bars, bottles of pop, and paper cups shot into the air. Eric tripped over his own feet and went over backward. When he scrambled up hastily, Gus had found the open pop bottle. As he had done so many times for the tourists at Ten-Day Watson's, Gus had the bottle in his mouth, his big head thrown back, and was drinking the contents. The building exploded in a roar of laughter, hand clapping, and whistling, and stomping. The applause drowned out the organ and drum.

Cliff heaved the pad, springboard, and trampoline aside and sprang to his feet. His face was streaked with dirt and twisted with rage. He rushed at Gus, the heavy-handled whip raised to strike. His foot struck a rolling pop bottle and both feet shot into the air. He let out a yell of fright, did a half somersault, arms and legs thrown wide, and landed on his back. The crowd howled and clapped and pounded their feet with glee. Cliff had jumped to his feet a second time when the clowns, Joe and Rusty, rushed the length of the room whooping and yelling. They gathered Cliff up in their arms and went galloping out. Cliff waved his fists and shouted into the din. The crowd applauded wildly.

Gus finished the bottle of pop, dropped it, and looked about curiously. He tilted his big nose and sniffed at Eric. Eric stood transfixed, horrified at what had happened. Then he picked up the chain and with Gus padding happily beside him led him out of the room.

Charlie Allen swung him about and hissed, "Get back in

there. Lead Gus around the room and come back here and take a bow before you come out the door. Go on! Go on!"

"I can't," Eric cried.

"You've got to. That crowd thinks this was an act. You've got to carry it off." He shoved hard candy into Eric's hand, "Give Gus one of these. Now get going, boy. Get moving!"

Eric started walking along in front of the jammed stands like one in a dream. Gus paced unconcernedly beside him, big nose questing for something to eat. Eric fed him a piece of candy and held another in his hand, which Gus kept reaching for, making grunting noises in his throat. The crowd began to applaud again.

Henry Marcel recovered from his shock and began shouting over the P.A. system. "Ladies and Gentlemen, from the wilds of the fabulous North, the greatest bear on earth — the one and only Gloomy Gus. With him is Eric Strong who raised Gus from a tiny cub to the immense size he now is."

Eric circled the room and the applause followed him. The organ boomed and the drum rolled. He came to the door again and Charlie shouted, "Take your bow! Turn around and bow!" Eric turned and bowed stiffly to the packed house. He put an arm around Gus's big neck and patted his head. Gus lifted his nose and whoofed mightily.

Eric led Gus outside, put him in his cage, closed the door, and leaned against it. He was shaking and his heart was pounding. Applause kept pouring from the building. He turned around and Cliff Marcel stood in front of him, feet braced apart, fists knotted. The streak of dirt was still smeared across his angry face, and his straight black hair hung over his eyes. "You did that on purpose," he raged. "You made me look like a fool." He lashed out suddenly. The punch drove Eric's head back against the cage bars. Cliff hit him again in the jaw. Then Eric ducked his head, charged into Cliff, and got his arms around the stockier boy. Eric's arms were long, his stringy muscles tough, and his hands hard from the summer work with Ten-Day Watson; but he had never been in a fight. He threw Cliff off with an awkward strength. When the stocky boy rushed again, Eric doubled his fist and threw it at Cliff's angry face. The punch jarred him to a stop. Eric threw another punch and another. Cliff sat down hard on the ground. Blood began to pour from his nose.

Then Charlie had his arms around Eric and was saying, "That's enough. That's enough."

Mr. Marcel helped Cliff to his feet. He handed the boy a handkerchief and said, "All right, you young roosters, to the truck. We're going to clear this up."

Inside the Marcel truck Eric sat stiffly on a chair, Charlie leaned against the wall, and Cliff let his nose bleed into a basin. Henry Marcel sat down and said, "Now, then, what happened in the ring? I couldn't see everything."

Cliff pointed at Eric and said angrily. "He caused the whole thing, Pa. You saw what he did."

"Tell me what he did."

"He deliberately stood where the bear could see him. Eric knew exactly what he'd do. He planned it."

Eric shook his head. "I didn't even know Gus was going to be shown tonight. I didn't plan anything. How could I?"

"You could have got out of the way," Cliff accused. "But no, you had to stand there like a dope. You could have gone out that little end door. You weren't twenty feet from it. But not you. You wanted to make me look like a fool. Well, nobody does that to me. Nobody!"

Henry Marcel looked at Eric. "What's your side of it?"

"I didn't see any door," Eric said. "I saw Gus come into the room and I was so surprised I just stood there and looked at him. I hadn't seen him for days. I didn't know what Cliff was going to do with him. And I didn't think with all those people he'd see me. I was opening a bottle of pop for a boy and Gus saw me holding the bottle just like I used to hold his sugar water bottle for him in the North." He smiled faintly. "He remembered!"

"He remembered because you've been sneaking out to see him when you're supposed to keep away, so he'd forget you," Cliff accused.

"Eric hasn't seen him," Charlie said. "And you've been around animals enough by now to know they don't forget easily or soon."

"So it was an accident," Henry Marcel said. "How did those clowns get out there so fast?"

"I saw what was happening and sent them out," Charlie said. "I thought it might pass off as part of the act and no one would get wise. It went over big. You heard the laughing and applause."

"I heard it. But we've got to be careful it doesn't happen again."

"Why?" Charlie asked.

"Why! It could have wound up in an awful mess, Charlie. You know that."

"It turned out a good act," Charlie said.

"It was an accident," Cliff said angrily.

"But a good act."

"Nobody taught him that. He just did it naturally," Cliff insisted.

"That's how some of the best acts come about. If you don't think this was good, listen." Charlie leaned back and opened the door.

The show was over. The organ was playing the exit march. There were voices and laughter as the crowd streamed past the truck in the dark. "Did you see the look on that trainer's face when the bear took off dragging him?" "And that kid falling down backward when the bear's nose hit the tray?" "How about him drinking that bottle of pop? I liked that." "Funniest thing I ever saw." "Was that bear big!" "Wow! Do you suppose he really is the biggest bear in the world?" "Who cares, he's big." "How about that kid walking him around the room. Man, I wouldn't do that."

"A good act," Charlie said quietly. "Fine entertainment. That's the job of a circus: to send people home laughing, happy, excited, talking about the things they've seen. That Gus act did it."

Henry Marcel scowled thoughtfully. The sounds of the

homeward-bound crowd kept coming through the door. Finally he nodded. "All right, we'll keep it. We'll make it the windup, the one we send them home on." He smiled; then, "You know, it really was good."

"I won't do it." Cliff wiped the last drop of blood from his nose and angrily shoved the pan aside. "I'm through with that bear. I won't be laughed at."

"I've got a lot of money in that bear," Henry Marcel said. "Transportation, advertising, feed, and what I have to pay Strong every week. It won't hurt you to put on this act."

"Pa, it will. I've got my own bear act with the blacks. It won't look good if I come out after that and do a falling-down comedy routine. No animal trainer would do that."

"He's got a point," Charlie said.

"Then what do we do?" Henry Marcel looked at Charlie. "It's a fine act and he's the only tame Kodiak in the world. I intend to use him."

"I can lead Gus in," Charlie said thoughtfully. "We've become pretty good friends. I'll put on a clown suit and he can drag me around. It won't hurt this game leg. We can do the whole act like it went off this evening."

Henry Marcel considered, black eyes studying Eric. "You think he can do it?" he asked Charlie.

"I know he can. This calls for no particular circus knowledge other than knowing the animal. And Eric raised Gus."

"He's got no outfit and I can't write him a contract this late in the season."

"I've got my old high-wire silver suit. We'll talk Edna into cutting it down to fit Eric. She's very good with a needle and thread. As for a contract, pay me what Eric would get. Ned Strong has never come through with his share for grub. Eric's pay should cover that with a few dollars left over for him. Okay, Eric?"

"Yes," Eric said.

"All right," Henry Marcel agreed. "How soon can you have that act ready to go on?"

"We'll go through a few rehearsals and be ready. A week,

maybe. This is a natural. We'd better move Gus's trailer cage up here."

"I go on ahead of this," Cliff said. "I won't follow a comedy bear act."

"Of course," Henry Marcel agreed. He glanced from Eric to Cliff. "As for you two roosters, this fight ends here. Understand? One troublemaker in a show can ruin it."

"Yes, sir," Eric said.

"Cliff," Henry Marcel warned, "you hear me? Shake hands."

Eric extended his hand. Cliff hesitated, then he gripped Eric's hand briefly and turned away.

Outside, Charlie said, "You sure graduated from candy butcher to performer in a hurry. Next season, you'll get a contract. How about that?"

"Charlie, I can't," Eric said quickly. "You know I can't. I don't know anything about performing."

"Don't have to. You do just what you did this evening."

"But in front of a thousand people. Tonight was an accident. I had to do that."

"You did it once," Charlie said, "you can do it again."

"It's different. I don't know anything about performing. I don't know how to act."

"You don't have to."

"I'd be scared to death with all those people looking."

"That's a good sign. The performers that are nervous beforehand always put on the best show. Just think you're back up north showing Gus off to the tourists."

"Maybe I'll do everything wrong."

"We'll rehearse plenty before we put it on. You leave it to old Charlie and quit worrying. You'll do fine."

"Well," Eric said, "all right." He thought of something and added, "You said there'd be money left over after paying our share of the grub."

"It won't make you rich."

"You keep it. Pa wouldn't let me have it."

"He don't need to know."

"He'll find out somehow."

"Then I'll keep it for you. When you want it, holler."

When they reached their truck, the last of the crowd had disappeared down the dark streets. The music had stopped and already the building was closed for the night. In the trucks, Eric knew, tired performers were crawling into their bunks for a few hours' sleep.

# - 10 -

CHARLIE ALLEN'S SUIT of silver spangles had not been worn in more than twenty years. He kept it neatly folded in mothballs, packed away in the bottom of an old truck with other paraphernalia of his wire-walking days. Eric slipped into the suit, and Charlie and Edna inspected him critically. Edna said, "Lengthen the legs two inches, the arms an inch, take two inches out of the waist, and it'll fit perfectly. You'll look mighty spiffy in this outfit."

"It'll spoil it for Charlie," Eric said.

"I'll never wear it again. How long will it take, Edna?"

"This isn't much of a job. Give me a day." She smiled at Eric as they left. "I'm glad you're handling Gus in the act."

Others spoke to Eric as they returned to their truck. Mario said, "If you have trouble making Gus behave, just call on Rose. She outweighs him. Good luck, Eric." Chet Olds said, "Congratulations, Eric. Last night was great." Billy Markson popped out of the chimps' truck and made an O of thumb and forefinger. "Nice going," he smiled.

Charlie said, "I told you they were nice people."

That morning Rose pushed Gus's trailer back and they hooked it on behind the truck. Eric was immediately out talking to Gus, scratching at his ears and rubbing under his chin. "I'm sure glad you're back," he said. "I've missed you." Gus rumbled in his chest and pressed his nose between the bars searching for food.

The next morning Edna brought the silver-spangled suit

back and it fit perfectly.

They waited until they reached the next location, a recreation building on a county fairgrounds, before they rehearsed the act. Charlie set the scene very carefully. "Eric, stand about here. No farther down the room than this and about fifteen feet out from the first row of seats." He chalked an X on the floor where Eric was to stand. "Now, the first mat here. This is the one I trip over. I want it lengthwise, so I can fall on it and not the floor. I've got to be careful to hit the mat on my good left hip. Let's have a chair here. Gus can drag me into it. Another mat here and a plain collapsible card table here to take the place of the trampoline. All this stuff piles up against my head and shoulders as Gus drags me. I let go of the chain here. Gus gets to you. You're holding up the bottle of pop so he can see it. We'll put a lot of dummy candy bars and pop bottles on your tray. Gus may not always lift up his nose high enough to hit the tray so you may have to help him. Carry it low and have one hand on the edge so that if he misses the bottom you can flip it in the air."

"Won't the people see if I do?"

"They'll be watching Gus, not you. With a little practice you can time it so close they'll never guess even if they are watching. And carry the tray tipped a little that way so the dummy bottles will fly away from him. You'll have the only good bottle in your hand. You've got to be sure that when you fall, you drop it right under Gus's nose where he can find it easy. Don't be in a hurry to get up. Roll around on the floor a little and give me time to finish my part. Now, Gus has found the bottle and is drinking it. I jump up, mad as a wet hen, grab the chair that's been dragged along, and rush at Gus as if to hit him. I've got to trip over my own feet and fall again, about here. Put another mat there. That's the signal for Joe and Rusty to dash in whooping and yelling and carry me out, waving my fists and shouting at Gus.

"Then you jump up, yank off your cap, skin out of your white coat and, presto, there you are in your silver spangles. You pick up Gus's chain and lead him slowly around the room so everyone gets a good look at him. Don't hurry. Remember, your job is to show off Gus. Circle the room twice so the M.C. has time to finish his spiel. When you get to the exit, turn around, face the crowd, and take your bow. You put your arm around Gus's neck the other night. They loved it. Do it again."

"Gee," Eric said, "I thought you just did a trick and that was all."

"Everything is timed, every move worked out in detail in advance, but you execute it so the audience never guesses. And, remember, always do it exactly the same way. Never change a trick even the least bit on an animal. They don't understand, become confused, and that's how trainers are sometimes injured. All right, let's go through it."

They rehearsed the trick again and again, and only the first time did Eric fail to drop the bottle of pop by seeming accident under Gus's nose. The last time they tried it with the music and drum. Henry Marcel gave his spiel and timed it to Eric and Gus's walk around the auditorium.

"Fine! Fine!" Henry Marcel clapped his hands. "How soon can we use it?"

"Give us a few more day's practice," Charlie said.

Eric had just returned Gus to the cage when his father came down the steps of the truck. He hadn't been up long and his eyes were red, his veined cheeks slack and puffy. He said, "I hear you're gonna be in some kinda act with that Gus bear."

"I don't do much."

"You gettin' paid for it?"

"I just lead Gus around the room so everybody can see him. You had anything to eat, Pa?"

"Don't change the subject on me. You gettin' paid?"

Eric nodded. "A little."

"How much? Come on, kid, how much?"

"Just enough to pay yours and Eric's grub bill," Charlie said behind Eric. "Henry Marcel gives it to me instead of Eric. Eric understands that. If you remember, Strong, I've been footing your bill ever since you came."

"Wasn't nothin' said 'bout grub when we come down."

"You've known it since the day you got here."

"Kid peddled pop and candy for it. He's helping you all the time."

"Everybody helps everybody else here. And Eric was a candy butcher just one night."

"Kid ain't supposed to work less'n he gets paid," Strong insisted.

"And you're not supposed to eat unless you pay your share," Charlie said.

"That's got nothin' to do with the kid gettin' paid."

"He's getting paid."

"Oughta be in hard cash."

"It would be if you drank a little less and paid your share of the grub."

"Don't tell me how to spend my money," Ned Strong said stiffly.

"I don't think anybody could," Charlie said.

"Now you're gettin' smart." Ned Strong walked away.

"I don't think he had anything to eat," Eric said worriedly.

"He couldn't eat now. Don't worry about it."

They went on that night right after Chet Olds' lion act. Eric was halfway down the auditorium and keeping well away from the customers so no one could ask him for a pop or candy. He was on the exact spot where he was supposed to be. He waited for Mr. Marcel's whistle and the music to bring Gus and Charlie in. He thought of the hundreds of pairs of eyes that would be on him in a minute. His throat was dry. His heart hammered painfully. He raised the bottle of pop and his hand was shaking. He was trying to remember all the things he was supposed to do when the whistle shrilled. The music blared, the snare drum rolled. Mr. Marcel's voice boomed into the room, "And now, Ladies and Gentlemen, from the wilds of Alaska, the greatest carnivorous animal on earth. The world's biggest and only tame Kodiak bear — the one and only Gloomy Gus!"

Gus padded into the room, head down, the lights laying

a golden sheen on his thick coat, the muscles rolling and bunching across his massive shoulders.

Charlie carried off his part of the act flawlessly. He stubbed his toe and went flat when Gus started to trot toward Eric. He was dragged into a chair, the card table, another mat. He yelled, kicked his legs, and waved his arms frantically. Gus's big nose hit the bottom of the tray and Eric reacted automatically exactly as they'd practiced all those long hours. Next, Charlie was being carried out by the clowns waving and shouting.

Gus went about the business with the bottle oblivious of the shouting and laughing. His calmness steadied Eric.

Eric jumped up, snatched off his cap, and peeled out of his white coat and stood revealed in Charlie's remodeled silver suit. He walked Gus twice around the room to steady applause and out the door. The organ swung into the exit march and Henry Marcel began his final speech.

Charlie clapped Eric on the back. "Good, good! You did fine." He patted Gus. "So did you. Now get him back in the cage, Eric, before the crowd starts coming out."

The act was good. Everyone in the show had congratulated them on a solid performance. Mr. Marcel was happy. But Charlie was not satisfied. "I wish he could do a couple of simple tricks," he said to Eric a couple of days later.

"I thought you didn't want him to become a performing bear."

"I don't mean like balancing on a ball, riding a scooter, or walking a plank the way Cliff wanted. I want something simple and natural. Walking twice around a big room with nothing else happening is too much walking. We need to break it up to make it a complete, well-rounded act."

"I never tried to teach him tricks," Eric said. "When he was little he'd stand on his hind legs and hold the milk bottle in his paws, but that's all. He did that naturally. I guess it was easier for him to handle the bottle that way."

"That's one of the secrets of being a good trainer," Charlie said. "You study the animal and learn what he does naturally. Then you take advantage of it. The paying customer thinks the trainer has actually taught the animal everything when he hasn't. Now, then, let's try something. Maybe Gus will remember, or maybe he'll do it naturally again." Charlie tied a bottle of pop to a stick, let Gus see it, then began raising it in the air as Gus reached for it. Gus followed the bottle up, rearing finally to his full height before Charlie let him have it. "Get a stick and punch him in the ribs just hard enough so that he recognizes it as a signal as he starts to go up for the bottle. Keep saying 'Up, Gus, up! Up!' until he gets it."

Soon they had Gus taking the bottle in his paws and rising to his full imposing height on signal.

"Good, good!" Charlie said. "Now if we had one more. Most anything would do." He was thoughtful a moment. "I've seen panhandling bears in Glacier National Park and Yellowstone sit up and beg tourists for food. It shouldn't be hard to teach Gus that."

They experimented. It took a great deal of patience, but finally they had Gus sitting on his haunches to beg for an apple the moment he saw it in Eric's hand. He held up his paws to receive the apple in what looked like a praying attitude and waited, little eyes on the apple. "We can use that," Charlie smiled. "Now we've got a well-rounded act."

That night when Eric led Gus around the auditorium, Mr. Marcel called over the P.A. system, "Gus, show the folks how tall you are." Eric took a bottle of pop from his pocket, pulled the cap, gave it to Gus, and said, "Up, Gus! Up!" Gus rose to his full height, held the bottle with his paws, and drank it to a burst of applause. They circled the ring and Mr. Marcel called, "Gus, show the folks how you beg." Eric immediately pulled the apple from his pocket and let Gus see it. Gus promptly sat back on his haunches, paws held under his chin. Eric waited a couple of seconds so the crowd was sure to see, then tossed Gus the apple to more applause.

Eric began to see posters of Gus and himself plastered to old buildings and in vacant store windows. In the small cities and towns there were articles and pictures in the local papers and spots on the local radio and television. They played to packed auditoriums, school gymnasiums, and fairground buildings. As it had been in Tatouche, Gus was the big attraction. Gus seemed to enjoy the bellowing organ and drum music. He'd swing his big nose up, little eyes going over the mass of people as he padded happily beside Eric. Charlie laughed, "Son of a gun, if I don't think that sometimes he's counting the house."

Cliff Marcel's black bear act still preceded them, but it was plain that Gus outshone them. Cliff knew it and became even more sullen and morose. He never spoke to Eric and he didn't come in to see the act.

Chet Olds patted Gus and said, "Even the cats can't compete with you. It's a good thing I'm leaving when my contract's up."

"What I need," Mario said soberly, "is hair on Jennie and Rose."

"I've got six horses with hair," Edna said, "but it doesn't help."

"Chimps are the smartest of all animals," Billy Markson complained, "but who cares when that Gloomy Gus shows up."

The last leaves fell from maple, willow, and oak. Often Eric woke to heavy frosts. But the winter rains held off and they continued to play to good crowds. Eric had become circus-minded. He lived from show to show and town to town. He learned to judge the towns and the crowds. But he could not get used to the constant moving, to a new town and new people every day or two. Charlie liked it and the rest of the circus people seemed to like it. It was a way of life with them. Eric wanted to belong somewhere, to put down roots. He wanted to meet the same people every day, do the same things, see the same streets and buildings, the same country. He missed Tatouche and Ten-Day Watson, Kenai, Sitka, and Friday Creek. He even missed Squeaky Joe Lucky, the Copper Lady, and his daily looks through the window of Eddie Lang's bar and George Summer's grocery. He turned the wristwatch over often and looked at the crudely scratched words, "To Eric from T.D.W.," and wondered if he'd ever see Tatouche and Ten-Day again.

Though Gus seemed to have adjusted well, Eric felt the bear would be happier in his far northern home.

Moving about did not bother his father. He'd locate the nearest tavern, where Eric could be sure to find him when they were ready to move on.

Henry Marcel had held out enough from Ned Strong's weekly check to pay himself back the cost of their transportation. Ned Strong began getting the full hundred dollars a week he'd been promised. When Charlie learned of it, he said, "You've got plenty of money now, Ned. You should be paying the weekly food bill and let Eric have a little of this money he's been earning."

"He don't need money. He spends all his time with that bear."

"He's been paying both your grub bills for weeks," Charlie pointed out.

"Do him good. He'll learn what money's for."

"Maybe you'd better learn, too," Charlie said sharply. "You'd better save some of that."

"When it comes in ever' week?"

"That well could dry up."

"Not likely but I'll worry about it," Ned Strong said and went off down the street.

The rain finally came. Once started it seemed to Eric it never stopped. Sometimes it was hard and pelting, at others it was a fine drizzle that lasted for days. Eric was more miserable than ever. The winters he'd known had been clean and white, the air biting and clear. Here the fog rolled in from a sea that was often more than a hundred miles away. The air was always damp and clammy. The cages, the animals, and sometimes the arena itself were wet. The crowds dwindled. They'd lie for days in some soggy vacant lot with no date to play or while waiting for the rain to let up so they could put on a show and fulfill a contract.

It was at one of these layovers that Cliff confronted Eric. He was coming back from Gus's cage late in the evening. Cliff materialized suddenly from behind one of the lion cages, grabbed Eric's arm, and jerked him about. His wet angry face was thrust close. "How's the big-shot performer?" he said harshly. "How's it feel to walk around the ring in silver spangles taking bows and seeing the write-ups in the papers and the posters stuck up about you and that bear? You like it, huh, big shot?"

"I'm no big shot," Eric said.

"I'll say you're not. You and that dumb bear and your penny-ante act are lucky. Plain lucky."

Eric pulled loose and started to walk away.

Cliff yanked him around again. "Don't walk away from me," he snapped. "I've been waiting for a chance to tell you this. I haven't forgot those sneaky little punches. Nobody does that to me and gets away with it. The only reason I don't smash your face is because we're on the road. Wait till we go into winter quarters. You and me are gonna settle this. We'll see how lucky you are then. Just so you don't forget..." He slammed both palms into Eric's chest. Eric stumbled back, tripped over the foot Cliff had slid behind his heel, and sat down hard in the mud. Then Cliff was gone.

When Eric entered the truck, Charlie looked up and said, "So you took a spill."

"Yes." Eric stripped off the muddy pants and asked, "Charlie, what's winter quarters?"

"Where we stay when not on the road. When the weather gets too bad and the crowds too small, we hole up someplace and wait for the bad weather to pass. It might be a vacant lot or open field. If we're lucky, maybe we find a big building where we can get the animals in the dry and work them a little while we wait for spring."

"What do you do during that time?"

"Repair and build new equipment, break in new acts, and rest up for next season. During that time Henry Marcel travels around the country lining up dates for next season and booking new acts to take the place of those that leave."

"Where will we go into winter quarters?"

"A little sawmill town up in the mountains. It's called Fir Crest. We wintered there last year. We rent a big barn a little way out of town."

"How soon will we be going up there?"

"Normally we'd have been up there a month ago. But Henry Marcel likes to run as long as he can. Now our bookings are running out and the weather's bad. We'll head south, out of this rain, any day now."

After a performance several nights later, a man followed and watched Eric return Gus to his cage. He was tall and lean, with a wind-tanned face and a shock of black hair. He asked, "Mind if I take a close look at your Gloomy Gus?" He bent over studying Gus a moment, then straightened. "When I saw those ads around town, I couldn't believe he was a tame Kodiak." He grinned. "He is though."

"You've seen Kodiaks before?"

"Every summer. I fish in the North. Got my own boat, the *Lady Lou*."

"Do you know where Tatouche is?" Eric asked eagerly.

"That old copper-mining town? I've put in there for supplies. I hear she got a new lease on life this summer with cruise ships and planes stopping."

"Yes," Eric said. "Do you know Ten-Day Watson"

"Crazy Watson? Saw him a couple of times. Don't know him, though."

"He's not crazy," Eric said stoutly. "He's my friend and Gus's. We're from Tatouche."

"Small world." He held out a hand. "Pete Clark. I live in Portland. I've been visiting a brother up here. Tell me, what happened to old Tatouche? Did they discover a new vein of copper?"

They sat down on a wooden bench under a makeshift covered walkway and Eric told Pete Clark about Gus and Ten-Day Watson, the cruise ships and the tourists. People hurried past huddled under umbrellas and bundled inside raincoats. Edna ran by, a cape thrown over her glittering costume. Joe and Rusty plopped along, oversized shoes flapping grotesquely in the rain puddles. Other performers scattered through the dripping night to their trucks. Charlie limped by, went into their truck, and closed the door. Darkness settled over the twenty trucks.

Finally Eric had told it all, right down to tonight. Pete Clark said, "Can't say I blame you for being homesick. That north country gets into a man. If I didn't have my home and family down here, I'd stay up there." He stood up and held out his hand. "A couple of old Alaskans like us could gab all night. You're going to freeze in that silver suit and I've got to get home."

"Will I see you again?" Eric asked wistfully.

"When are you leaving?"

"Tomorrow morning. We're heading south."

Pete Clark started to shake his head, then changed his mind and said, "I think you will, Alaska. Good night."

Eric searched for Pete Clark's tall figure while they were packing next morning. Finally they were ready to leave and Clark had not come. Half the trucks had already pulled out. Charlie said, "We'll wait a few minutes, then we'll have to go."

"Yes." Eric stood in the rain and watched. Chet Olds pulled out with his lions, waving as he went by. The truck with the chimps followed. Eric was about to get back into their truck when he spotted Pete Clark far down the street. He ran to meet him.

"Hello, Alaska," Pete smiled. "I almost didn't make it. My brother's car wouldn't start. So you're all ready to pull out. I'm leaving this morning, too."

"You're going north?"

"Not right away. But in a few weeks. Do you realize spring is less than six weeks away?"

"I hadn't thought about it. We just move and set up and knock down, and move and set up again. I guess I'll never see the North again."

"You will, if you want to."

"Do you really believe that?"

"I sure do. You can get anything if you want it bad enough. But you've got to keep thinking about it. Got to keep it right in front of your mind all the time. Now, me, I wanted to go North, I made it. I wanted a forty-foot seiner. Got a forty-six footer instead. But you've got to want it bad, and you've got to keep trying."

"Then maybe I'll make it," Eric smiled. "Will you say hello if you see Ten-Day Watson?"

"I'll make a point of it."

They talked a few minutes longer. Then Pete Clark said, "I think your friend is getting a little anxious, and I've got to be going, too." He held out his hand. "Say good-bye to Gus for me. If you both get to where you can't stand it down here, come over to Portland. My home's on Marine Drive, number 1620, right on the Columbia. The *Lady Lou* is moored in the backyard. I'll take you and Gus north with me."

"Do you mean it?"

"You know one Alaskan wouldn't lie to another?" Pete Clark smiled.

"Gee, thanks," Eric said. "I'll remember." He watched Pete Clark walk back down the street, his collar turned up against the lash of the rain.

116

# - 11 -

IT TOOK TWO WEEKS to work their way south toward Fir Crest. They played their last date in the rain in a small town at the foot of the mountains. The next morning the circus broke up. Those that were leaving pulled out. Some would return in six or eight weeks to join them on the spring tour. Others, like the Marletto Brothers, the two clowns, Joe and Rusty, Ken Tucker of the slide-for-life, and Billy Markson and his chimps, were joining other circuses to tour the South.

Mario and his elephants, Edna and her liberty horses, the two Marcels with Cliff's black bears, and Charlie's truck with Gloomy Gus were all that was left. Henry Marcel led this little caravan into the timbered mountains toward Fir Crest.

Fir Crest was a small one-street town. Its principal industries were a large sawmill and a railroad roundhouse.

The place Henry Marcel had rented was on an abandoned logging road a mile out of town. It consisted of a couple of acres to park their trucks and a huge old barn. The cages were put inside the barn against one wall. Jennie and Rose were tethered to a chain that was held to the floor by iron stakes driven into the ground. In another section of the barn there were stables for Edna's liberty horses.

A load of hay was brought in for the horses and elephants. Mr. Marcel made arrangements at several food stores in nearby towns for day-old bread, lettuce, apples, and grapes for the bears. Then everyone settled down to rest up and make ready for spring. Edna repaired the horses' harness and

117

worked them intermittently trying out a new act. Mario did not work Rose and Jennie, preferring to let them rest. Eric and Charlie did not work Gus.

"He'll remember, don't worry," Charlie said. "Let him rest and be fresh for spring." So on the good days they tied him out and let him eat grass, which he loved. Cliff worked the black bears every day, but he insisted Eric leave the barn before he'd bring them out.

Eric remembered Cliff's threat about finishing their fight and expected the stocky boy to jump him at the first opportunity. He was not afraid, Eric told himself. The thought worried him because he saw no reason to fight. But he was not going to avoid Cliff. If he was cornered, he'd fight. How well, he didn't know. He guessed Cliff had been in many fights. Eric knew by the scowls he got that Cliff was waiting for a time when neither Marcel nor Charlie would be around to interfere.

Eric's father found a tavern at the outer edge of town and hiked down every day. It was always late at night when he returned. Several times he did not come back until the next day.

Eric said to Charlie, "We're not on the road now, so you're not getting that money for Gus and my act to pay for our grub. You've got to get it from Pa. He's still getting that hundred a week from Mr. Marcel."

Charlie shook his head. "I don't understand Henry Marcel doing a thing like that. But you're right. I'll talk to him."

Ned Strong scowled and rubbed a hand across his mouth. "Marcel never said nothin' 'bout me paying for grub."

"I'm paying it and I'm telling you now. Eric was paying it until we came up here. Now he can't. It's your turn. Come through, Ned."

"I don't eat as much as you and the kid."

"That's true enough."

"Charlie does all the cooking, Pa," Eric said. "That counts for something."

"Keep your oar outa this, kid."

"Give, Ned!" Charlie held out a hand. "I can't afford to feed you. I'm not getting paid now either. And don't tell me

118

you've spent it all."

Ned Strong rubbed a hand across his mouth again. "I'll give you twenty a week," he mumbled.

Charlie hesitated, studying Ned Strong. "All right," he said finally. "Give."

Ned Strong grudgingly counted money into Charlie's palm. "That hundred was supposed to be all mine."

"That's between you and Henry Marcel. He pays you every Saturday night. I want mine Saturday night, not Sunday or Monday. Saturday."

"Sounds like you don't trust me," Ned Strong said stiffly.

"Saturday night, Ned."

Ned Strong drew himself up. "You'll get it, tightwad," and walked out.

Gus went to sleep and didn't move for a week. He woke up for a couple of days, then went to sleep for another short period. "That's about as close as they come to a winter sleep in captivity down here," Charlie commented.

Eric and Charlie spent their time cleaning up, repairing and repainting the popcorn machine, candy-floss machine, making new carriers for the snow cones and trays for the candy butchers. They patched the uniforms. Eric was surprised at how good Charlie was with a needle and thread. They ran the truck into the small outbuilding and overhauled the motor.

March was gone and they were well into April. Johnny-jump-ups and trilliums were blooming. The heaviest rains had slacked off. There were days of fine mists and periods of pale sunlight. Willow and maple buds were swelling.

Henry Marcel and Cliff left together for an indefinite time. "Don't know how long we'll be gone," Henry Marcel explained to Charlie. "Ten days, maybe two weeks. Cliff wants to hunt up another bear. I've got to line up acts to replace those that won't return. And I'll try for some late spring bookings. It's all yours here." Cliff gave Eric a hard stare, then got into the cab that had come out from town for them.

"I see Cliff hasn't forgotten that punch in the nose," Charlie observed.

"No."

"Too bad. A circus is no place for grudges."

The Marcels were gone over two weeks, and when they returned Cliff had not found another bear. But Henry Marcel had signed on six new acts and had a solid six weeks of bookings.

A week passed. The small buds on the maple and willow opened. The first leaves appeared. Charlie hiked down to Fir Crest for groceries. Eric lay in his bunk reading. His father was still asleep when Mr. Marcel came to the truck. He stared down at the sleeping man and said annoyed, "I want to talk to him. I was sure he'd be up. It's almost evening."

"He didn't get in until this morning," Eric said.

"When he wakes up, get him as sober as you can and bring him to my truck. I've got to talk to him."

Eric's father woke an hour later and Eric had hot coffee, bacon, and potatoes for him. Ned Strong sat on the edge of his bunk and mumbled, "You're gettin' supper pretty early."

"It's for you," Eric said. "Mr. Marcel was here anhour ago. He wants to talk to you."

"What's that got to do with cookin' now."

Eric bit his lip. "He said he wanted you sober."

"You sayin' I'm drunk, kid?"

"It's what he said, Pa."

"Well, I can't eat that stuff. Gimme the coffee."

"Pa, Mr. Marcel said he had to talk to you. It's important."

"Important. He said that, huh? He had to talk to me?" Ned Strong straightened and slapped a hand against his knee. He began to grin. "That's it! By golly! I'll just bet that's it. One of them big outfits has heard about us. Some big circus wants that old Gloomy Gus." He became excited. "Know what that means, kid? Five hundred a week. It's 'bout time, too. Yessiree-Bob, I knew one of 'em was bound to hear 'bout us."

"He didn't say that, Pa."

His father shook his head emphatically. "That's it, all right. We'll be shakin' this two-bit show and goin' to one of them big ones. Think of that, kid. No more sleepin' in a busted-down truck. We're gonna live."

"But, Pa, he didn't mention anything about a circus."

"Said he had to talk to me, didn't he?" He was showing more life than Eric had seen in weeks. He gulped down the hot coffee and reached for his hat.

"Pa, you haven't had a decent meal for days," Eric said.

"This here news is better'n a steak." His father jammed on his hat and went out.

Eric followed.

Mr. Marcel opened the door and said, "Well, Ned. I've been wanting to talk to you. Come in." He closed the door in Eric's face. Eric turned away, then stopped. Charlie had told him their chances of getting in with one of the big circuses left were almost nil. Voices came clearly through the thin metal wall.

Eric's father said, "So one of them big outfits wants the bear, huh?"

"That's not what I want to talk to you about."

"You ain't heard from one of them big outfits?"

"Sit down and listen to me, Ned. Now, then, I've been paying you a hundred dollars a week. I can't afford it. We're not taking in a dime now, and we won't for the next month or so. I want to buy Gloomy Gus. I'll give you seven hundred and fifty dollars for him."

"Why, I'll make most that much in a week in one of them big shows," Ned Strong said indignantly. "Nothin' doin'. That Gus ain't for sale. Just wait till one of them big shows hears about him."

"They're not going to hear."

"They got to, with all them write-ups and pictures in store windows and things."

"No," Henry Marcel said. "There aren't any big shows left."

"Whatta you mean? You told me. I don't like that kind of talk."

"There's no big shows left, Ned," Henry Marcel said

121

again. "They're all out of business. If you'd stayed sober you'd have heard that by now."

"But you told me…"

"Now I'm telling you. All the big shows have folded — gone broke or quit. Only little ones like ours are left."

There was silence. Eric could visualize his father trying to understand this startling statement.

Then, "What about movies? What about that Hollywood talk?"

"Hollywood's got all the animals they need. They've got to have trained animals that can act. Gus can't act. Forget Hollywood."

"You lied to me!" Ned Strong's voice was angry. "Everythin' you told me was a pack of lies."

"That's one way of looking at it," Marcel said. "The other is that we're both men. My job was to make as good a deal for my circus as possible. Yours was to get all you could for your bear. I offered you a contract and you turned it down. You figured you might gouge somebody else for more money. You'd have left me flat without a moment's notice. If you'd taken my contract, I'd have been stuck for that hundred a week for a year. Without it I'm not. I figure we're even."

"You had this whole thing figured out ahead of time," Ned Strong accused.

"No such thing," Marcel said. "I'd planned to buy the bear. Then I saw you wouldn't sell and I discovered you were nothing but a drunken bum who'd gouge me to the limit. I didn't make you drink. I even sobered you up so I could talk to you. You can blame yourself for the fix you're in."

"You ain't gettin' away with this, you crook!" Ned Strong shouted. "I'll wreck your stinkin' circus. I'll take the bear, and me and the kid'll leave."

"You do that," Marcel said, "and how will you eat? Where'll you go? You've spent every dime I've given you."

"I'll borrow to get back North."

"Who'd loan you money, Ned? Look at yourself in the mirror. Who'd loan that face money?"

"You crooked me!"

"You crooked yourself. If you'd saved your money, you'd have enough to get back North. You're not freeloading off me any longer while we're in winter quarters. Seven-fifty will get you and Eric home."

"The bear's worth more."

"Not to me."

"He's been packin' 'em in."

"Because he's a novelty. People want to see the 'biggest bear on earth, the world's only tame Kodiak.' If we go over the same route next season, he won't draw all these people because they've seen him once. Ask Charlie Allen if I'm not right."

"I could make more'n seven-fifty in Tatouche, just lettin' folks look at him."

"You're not in Tatouche. Seven-fifty for your bear or get out."

"He's worth double."

"Not to me. Not to any circus man. Seven-fifty, Ned."

"You're robbin' me."

"You and a bottle robbed yourself."

Ned Strong hedged. "I ain't sure I got a right to sell that Gus bear."

"Don't try to crawl out of it."

"I tell you I'm not sure."

"What do you mean? You own the bear, don't you?"

"He's Eric's bear."

"Eric's your son, so it's your bear. What you say goes."

"That ain't quite right. Sellin' somethin' kinda brings in legal things."

"What's that mean?"

"Means I ain't sure I can sell 'em. Might cause trouble."

"What kind of trouble? What're you giving me? Quit beating around the bush and say what you mean."

"Said it. I ain't sure I got a right to sell that bear."

"Don't try to pull anything on me, Ned. I've forgotten more tricks than you'll ever know."

"I tell you it might cause trouble with the kid."

"What kind of trouble?"

"I wish I knew." Ned Strong sounded worried. "I been thinkin' about it a long time."

"I'll bet. In every bar you sit in," Marcel said. "Come off it, Ned. As an actor you're pretty bad. You've never shown the least fatherly interest in Eric."

"That's what they said in Tatouche, too. And them that didn't say it was thinkin' it. I could tell. For fifteen years I knew it." Eric had never heard his father sound so bitter. "Fifteen years I supported that kid, fed 'im, bought his clothes."

"What's wrong with that?" Marcel asked.

"Would you do it for Cliff it he wasn't your kid? Would you?" Ned Strong demanded.

Eric held his breath. There was a long silence, then Marcel asked curiously, "You saying Eric's not your son, Ned?"

"I didn't say that."

"I think you did. You'd better level with me, Ned."

There was another silence. Then Ned Strong's voice said reluctantly, "He ain't my kid — not exactly."

"He is or he isn't." Marcel's voice was a pry digging in. "Which is it, Ned?"

Eric pressed against the cold side of the truck. "I ain't never told this to anybody, you understand?" Ned Strong began reluctantly. "But every time I've looked at that kid for fifteen years I've thought of it. Years ago his pa and me was partners in a mine up in the Kantishna. Eric's ma died. One day we had a cave-in and his pa was killed. It was an accident, but I couldn't prove it. It could have looked bad. I took the kid and went to Tatouche."

"Nobody asked questions about the cave-in or what happened to your partner?"

"Wasn't anybody to ask. We was miles out in the wild country. Practically nobody ever went there. I didn't see no sense tellin' him and maybe kickin' up a fuss."

"How about in Tatouche?"

"Nobody knew there."

"Then you can sell Gloomy Gus to me and quit worrying." When there was no answer, Marcel said, "You haven't any choice."

"You'd tell what I told you."

"I don't have to. Maybe you killed him. Maybe you were just careless. Or it could have been an accident like you say. After all these years nothing could be proved."

"That's right."

"The point is," Marcel continued, "you're broke and I won't let you freeload any longer. You've got to sell to me. I'm your only buyer."

Eric crept away from the side of the truck. He was shaking and his mind was racing. Now he understood many things.

Then Eric thought of Gus. If Ned Strong wasn't his father, he had no right to sell Gus. Gus was his. He had to keep Marcel from getting Gus. Perhaps if he told Charlie the whole story he could help. But Ned Strong and Henry Marcel could deny there was such a story, and even Charlie might doubt him. After all he was only a boy. He couldn't prove what he'd heard. There was only one way. He and Gus had to get out. But how?

He remembered Pete Clark, the Alaska fisherman. Pete had said, "If you both get to where you can't stand it down here, come over to Portland. I'll take you and Gus north with me." That was the answer. But he had to hurry. His father — rather, Ned Strong — might come to the barn any minute.

Eric ran toward the barn wondering how long it would take to get used to thinking of Ned Strong as not his father.

He didn't turn on the lights for fear someone might come to investigate. He made out the bulks of Jennie and Rose. Cracks of light came from the room at the far end of the barn where the horse stables were. He heard Edna talking to her horses. She was feeding and bedding them down. He dared not move. One of the elephants might take alarm in the dark and bellow. He heard the rustle of straw, the rattle of a can, as Edna dumped grain in the horses' boxes. After what seemed a long time the light went out and he heard her open and close the stable door.

He waited another minute, then moved carefully along the wall to Gus's cage. Gus's keen ears and nose told him Eric was coming. He was up and pressed against the bars. Eric reached through the bars and patted the big head. "Be quiet," he whispered.

Searching for some tidbit, Gus sniffed at Eric's hands. Eric dug into his pocket and gave him his last piece of hard candy. Gus chomped on it, smacking his lips. "Not so loud," Eric whispered. His groping hand found Gus's chain hanging on the wall. He was fumbling at the cage latch when the barn was flooded with light.

Ned Strong stalked across the floor. "I had a hunch you mighta come here when you wasn't at the truck. What do you think you're doin'?"

"You've got no right to sell Gus," Eric blurted.

"So you got big ears."

Ned Strong's voice was dangerously calm.

Anger rushed through Eric, smothering fear and caution. This was the man who had bullied, abused, and used him for years. "You're not my father. You're just a drunken tramp! A nothing! You've got no rights over Gus and me."

Ned Strong's big hand smashed into Eric's mouth. It drove his head against the bars of the cage. The hand came again and again. Eric's knees buckled. He tasted blood. He sprawled face down in the dirt, sick and dizzy. He got shakily to hands and knees. Ned Strong looked over him, bloated face twisted with rage. An elephant hook, a tool with which Mario trained the elephants lay on the floor by Eric's hand. It had a wooden shaft about three feet long with a dull steel hook on the end. Eric grabbed it and surged to his feet. He slashed at Strong's face with all his strength. The hook sent him stumbling back. Eric struck a second time. Ned Strong collapsed and lay still.

Eric dropped the elephant hook and ran to Gus's cage. He opened the cage, got the chain around Gus's neck, and led him out. He turned off the lights, opened the barn door, and Charlie said, "I was wondering why the lights were on." He saw Gus and asked, "What goes on?"

Eric poured out the story.

"Maybe I killed him. He's awful still."

"Let's go see." Charlie snapped on the lights and bent over Ned Strong. After a minute he rose and said, "You conked him pretty good. But he'll come out of it soon. There's nothing to worry about. So the drunken bum isn't your pa after all. I'm not surprised, and you ought to be glad." Charlie snapped off the lights. "We don't want somebody coming to investigate," he explained. "Now, what's this about you leaving?"

"Gus and I are going to Portland. Pete Clark, the fisherman, remember him? He said he'd take us north with him this spring if we wanted to go."

"If Ned Strong's not your pa, they can't take Gus away from you. In fact, you can make it hot for anybody that tries," Charlie pointed out.

"You believe me," Eric said, "but who else would? Ned Strong would deny it because he's afraid of something about that cave-in. Mr. Marcel will say I made it up because he wants Gus. I can't prove a thing."

"Maybe you're right," Charlie agreed. "But how do you know Pete Clark wasn't just talking, being friendly to a lonely boy?"

"He meant it. He said so."

"You figure to hike all the way to Portland? Alone, you could do it easy, but not leading a bear. The first person that saw you would notify the police."

"We'll keep out of sight."

"How'll you do that? It's a hundred miles away."

"I don't know. But we will. We've got to. We're going home to Tatouche."

"You'll be caught."

"We won't be any worse off than if we hadn't tried."

Charlie studied him in the dark for a moment. "I guess

so. I'd try at your age, too. It's a crazy idea. But with luck and a lot of fight, crazy ideas sometimes work out. You might make it. You just might."

Ned Strong groaned. Charlie bent, grabbed him, and started dragging him toward Gus's cage.

"What are you doing?" Eric cried.

"Helping you." Charlie stuffed Ned Strong's half-conscious body into the cage, closed the door, and locked it. "You need a head start, so we've got to keep this character quiet for a few hours." He led the way outside. "How much money have you got?"

"None."

"Wait here." Charlie ran limping to the truck. He returned and shoved a handful of bills at Eric. "Here's a hundred dollars. It's all the cash I've got right now. It's about what I managed to save for you out of your earnings for the act. Be careful, boy. Be careful. Stay off the main highways and keep Gus out of sight." He patted Gus's big head and shook hands with Eric. "Keep heading north. So long."

"How'll you keep Ned Strong from yelling when he comes to?" Eric asked.

"You leave that to me," Charlie smiled. "I haven't been in the circus for forty years for nothing. Get going now. Move, boy!" He limped away in the darkness toward the barn.

Eric took Gus past their truck and headed into a little used trail that he knew led past the town. He rounded a corner and came face to face with Cliff Marcel. Both boys stopped in surprise not ten feet apart. Eric knew this was the opportunity Cliff had been waiting for. His one chance of getting away was gone. To sound the alarm and get them caught was the kind of revenge Cliff would love. He was licked.

"So," Cliff straightened, "you're taking off, running away."

Eric said nothing.

Cliff took his hands from his pockets and doubled his fists. "I've owed you a licking for a long time."

Gus tugged at the chain reaching for a grass clump, and

Eric held on with both hands.

Cliff finally returned his hands to his pockets. "I'm going to let you off. Know why? Because you're running away. That bear of yours has been hogging the whole show because he's half as big as an elephant. Not because he's good. I want you out of the show. Understand? There's only room for one bear act and that's going to be mine. You're saving yourself a licking by sneaking off tonight. Go ahead, beat it! I don't care where. Just so it's a long ways from the Marcel and Son Circus. Don't worry. I won't say a word to Pa about your leaving." Cliff stepped aside with mock courtesy and waved down the dark trail. "Get moving. I hope you travel fast and far because Pa'll miss you in the morning and start looking."

Eric passed Cliff without a word. Behind him Cliff began whistling as he went on toward his father's truck. Eric felt like whistling too. He patted Gus's head bobbing beside him. "We're going home, Gus," he said. "We're going home!"

# PART III

❄

# A Long Journey

# - 12 -

ERIC AND GUS skirted Fir Crest, came out a mile north of town, and entered the blacktop road. Eric soon learned that by sticking to the center of the road they made time because Gus could not be constantly reaching for grass clumps or sniffing at some succulent plant. Eric kept pulling on the chain to hurry him along. "Come on, they'll be after us soon. We've got to get as far away as we can and hide. You want to get back to Ten-Day's as much as I do, don't you?"

At intervals, they dodged into the fringing brush when headlights appeared far ahead of them or behind them. They'd been several hours on the road when the police car from Fir Crest passed, its spotlight probing the brush along both sides. Eric wondered what had happened back at the barn that they should be missed so soon. A fine rain began falling and a chill wind blew across the logged-off hills and bit into him.

Several hours later, the road melted into the four-lane superhighway. Even at this hour the traffic was heavy. They crouched in the brush at the edge of the highway, and Eric waited for a break when no traffic came from either direction. Finally there was a hole. Eric rushed out dragging Gus with him and scooted across.

They had to keep going north. They headed into dark, soggy fields and through scattered patches of timber and came to a swift-running stream. Eric wandered along the bank looking for a log or shallow spot. He found none. Finally he plunged in and waded waist deep, with Gus surging along beside him. Again they crossed open fields and woods. They were constantly running into barbed-wire fences. Several times Eric found a gate that let them through. Or he stood on the wire and bent it down with his weight until Gus could plod over. Sometimes he pried the staples loose with a stick, let the wire down, and crossed, then hammered the staples back with a rock.

His wet feet and the fine rain chilled Eric to the bone. It didn't bother Gus. He shook water from his coat and padded along.

At the edge of a patch of timber they stumbled on to an old building. Eric led Gus inside out of the rain. It had a dirt floor and there were a couple of stalls at one end. He found a pile of loose straw. Gus walked into the middle of it and lay down with a gusty sigh. Eric curled up against Gus's solid back to get what warmth he could and pulled straw over him. He listened to the whisper of the wind through the trees and the beat of rain on the roof. Finally the heat from Gus's big body came through to him.

Eric awoke to a chill, gray morning. Sometime while he'd slept the wind and rain had quit. His clothing was almost dry, and here under the straw against Gus's big back he felt warm and comfortable. He lay looking out the broken door. This building hadn't been used for a long time. It was weather-grayed and some of the side boards were partially rotted. Light came through cracks in the old shake roof, but the floor was dry. The straw under which he lay was black with age.

Last night's urgency finally shook him fully awake. He stood up and brushed the straw from his clothing. He pulled on the chain and said, "Come on, Gus. Let's go." Gus heaved out of the straw and stood yawning hugely and blinking his small eyes. He lifted his big nose and sniffed at Eric. "I'm hungry, too," Eric said. "We'll find something as soon as we can." They headed into the soggy morning. Their northerly direction took them through the grove of trees.

They came out the far side into a long, flat meadow where a dozen black and white cows were feeding. Eric was about to start across when his eyes caught a movement on the far side. A man and a dog came out of the brush and headed toward the cattle. The man waved his arm toward the cattle and his voice drifted across the still morning, "Go get 'em, Nick."

The dog was off like a streak. He circled the cows barking at the top of his lungs. The cows bunched and started to trot toward the man. The dog ranged back and forth behind them keeping them moving. One cow broke away and galloped across the field straight toward Eric and Gus. She came to an abrupt halt not twenty feet away. She stared at Gus with big round eyes, shook her head, and snorted at the strange bear smell. She flapped her ears and stomped her feet, not sure what she had found.

The man whistled and waved his arm toward them. The dog raced for the cow. Eric knew the dog would see them and begin to bark. The man would come to investigate. He looked about frantically for a stick or rock to throw at the cow. There was nothing. He started forward to shoo her away, then stopped. The dog would see him. The dog was coming straight at them in great leaps. Then, for no apparent reason, the cow bolted. The dog veered to intercept her and sent her scampering back to the herd.

They stayed in the brush until cattle, dog and man had disappeared. Then they hurriedly crossed the meadow and entered the brush on the far side. An hour later they came to another narrow country road that wandered in the general direction they were traveling. Eric followed it, keeping close to the edge where they could duck into the brush at the first sound of an approaching car. Gus was hungry and kept trying to stop to eat grass and dig for roots. Eric yanked on the chain and urged him along. Finally Gus seemed to understand and padded along rapidly at Eric's side. Eric spotted several houses ahead built close to the road. They entered the brush, detoured around, and came into the road further on. A dog dashed out of the brush and rushed at them, barking. Gus whirled to meet the dog, ears laid back, teeth bared. Eric grabbed up a stick. Luckily it caught the dog in the side. He ran away howling.

During the next several miles a half-dozen cars and a closed van forced them into the brush. At the rate they were traveling, Eric realized, it was going to take days to reach the city. The closer they got, the thicker the traffic would be. If by some miracle they avoided detection, they had to travel streets lined with houses and filled with people. There must be another way.

He looked after the closed van. There went the perfect solution. About three or four hours in one of those with Gus out of sight and they could breeze right into Portland down to Marine Drive without anyone knowing. But how could he get a truck? He thought of the hundred dollars in his pocket. He could hire a truck. Now all he needed was the right truck and driver.

Gus again began trying to snatch chunks of grass as they went along. Finally Eric pulled off the road, found a cleared spot thick with grass, and sat down to let Gus feed. He was getting hungry himself, and listening to Gus snip off the grass clumps and chew noisily made the saliva run in his mouth. When Gus's side began to push out and he became choosy, Eric rose and pulled him back to the road.

It was almost noon when the country road they were following joined the expressway. From the safety of screening brush Eric studied the four-lane highway. Several hundred yards ahead there was a junction where the four lanes were crossed by another highway. A restaurant and grocery store stood at the junction. Several big vans were parked beside the restaurant.

Eric tied Gus to a tree well back from the road and went to the store. He bought four loaves of bread, a pound of cheap hard candy, and a pound of wieners. He looked for apples or grapes for Gus but there were none.

When he returned to Gus, he tore open the bread and gave Gus all but six slices. He ate four slices and half the pound of wieners. He treated himself to a piece of hard candy

135

and gave Gus two. He stuffed the remaining bread and wieners in his jacket pocket and returned to the road where he could watch the diner and store. A third truck had driven in and, as Eric watched, a fourth pulled off the highway. This was a truck stop where drivers liked to eat and take a break.

Here was the place to find the truck to take them into the city. But he could not lead Gus there in broad daylight. There'd be a lot of questions. Someone might call the police. He glanced at his watch. It was after three o'clock. In several hours it would be dark. Then he could lead Gus within a few feet of the diner without detection and choose his truck and driver without creating a disturbance.

He returned to Gus and found he'd settled down by the tree, big head on forepaws about to take a nap. Eric sat beside him and patted his head. "You're full and now you want a nap," he said. "Me, too." He was tired after their long hike, and the traffic on the expressway was a steady droning sound that lulled him to sleep.

Eric awoke shivering. The light was almost gone from the day. Gus had eaten more grass and was sniffing the remainder of the bread and wieners in his pocket. He made himself another sandwich and gave the rest to Gus.

Dusk settled in. Eric unchained Gus and they made their way toward the lighted diner. The store was closed for the night. They moved down close and Eric tied Gus behind a thin fringe of trees.

Several big freight trucks sat before the diner, and through the windows Eric saw the drivers inside eating at the counter. One was an older man, who looked sober. He ate steadily, his eyes on his plate. The second trucker was young. His cap was shoved on the back of a blond head and he was talking and laughing with the waitress. That was the one he'd ask for a lift.

The two men came from the diner together. The young man headed for the truck parked farthest away in the dark. He was climbing into the cab when Eric asked, "Mister, are you going to Portland?"

The driver looked around. "Oh, hello, kid. Yeah, I'm heading for Portland."

"Can I ride with you?"

The young fellow shook his head. "Not a chance."

"I don't mean for nothing. I can pay."

The driver shoved his cap on his blond head and studied Eric thoughtfully. "I'd take you for nothing if I dared." He pointed at the door. "See that. No riders. The company put that there and they mean it. This's a Western Freight Liner Truck and 'no riders' is company policy. I couldn't carry you no matter how much you paid."

"I didn't know." Eric turned away disappointed.

"Wait a minute," the driver said. "You wanta get to Portland pretty bad?" And when Eric nodded, he said, "All right, I'll tell you how to do it. Don't ask any of the big rigs like this one or the one up ahead. These tractor-trailer outfits belong to big companies and they all have the same 'no riders' policy. Look for a gyppo driver, a guy that owns just one truck and does his own driving around the country picking up loads wherever he can. Gyppos don't have the 'no riders' rule. They make their own. That's your best bet."

"How do I tell a gyppo?"

"They won't be big tractor-trailer rigs like this. They'll mostly be small trucks, no trailer at all, and they won't have all this fancy printing on the sides. You can tell 'em easy. Fact is, a friend of mine should pull in here in about half an hour. He's got a red truck, kind of old. It's got REID painted on the front and both sides in big white letters. Nothing else, just REID. Jim Reid's a gyppo, a nice guy. Tell him Dave Ford said to give you a lift." He slammed the cab door and started the motor. As he pulled away he called back, "Tell him I said to get rid of that cracker box and come drive a real rig with me."

Eric returned to Gus to wait. Gus was digging in the earth. He'd found some succulent roots and was chomping away industriously. Eric said, "Don't you ever get enough to eat?" Gus glanced up, then cleared his nostrils with a mighty blast.

There was a lot of traffic at the diner. At intervals big vans thundered in and stopped with a sighing of brakes. Pickups and trucks came and went. An hour passed and no old red truck with REID painted on the side appeared. Eric was about to give up and begin looking for another independent when an old truck rattled into the shadows near him and the driver climbed out and entered the diner. No color showed in the dark, but the name REID was plainly visible. It was about the size of one of the circus trucks, Eric guessed, but older. He looked through the diner window at the man sitting at the counter. He was young, about Dave Ford's age, and he wore a leather jacket and a cap pushed back on a mass of curly black hair. He was talking and laughing with another trucker. He had his dinner and came out, whistling.

Eric met him at the truck. He smiled and said, "Hi, kid."

"Are you Jim Reid?" Eric asked.

"Right the first time. How'd you know?"

"Dave Ford told me the kind of truck you drove."

"I can imagine what he said. You a friend of Dave's?"

"No, sir. Mr. Ford said you'd give me a ride into Portland."

"So that's it." Jim Reid lost his smile. "Oh, no you don't, kid. That's been tried before. You hang-around and listen to these drivers and pick up some names and start tossing 'em around to every driver that comes by until one falls for your story and gives you a lift. It don't work on this guy." He pulled the door open and swung up to the cab.

For a moment Eric felt lost, then he remembered and said, "Dave Ford said to tell you to get rid of that crackerbox and come with him and drive a real rig."

Jim Reid stepped down from the cab and stood over Eric. "Maybe I got you wrong. That's Dave's and my private argument. I take it back. You know him."

"He said he couldn't take me because of company policy. But that you could, and that you were a real nice guy."

"Mighty decent of him to add that," Reid observed. He took off his cap and scratched his head. "You ain't runnin' away from one of them boys' schools? Anybody that'd give

138

one of those kids a lift would be in real trouble."

"I've got to get to Portland to meet a man," Eric said. "I — I'm going on a boat. I'm going home."

"That don't tell me much. You could still be some kind of runaway."

"I'll explain as we go along," Eric said. "Then if you don't like it you can kick me out."

Reid grinned suddenly and slapped his cap back on his head. "Fair enough. Come on."

"I've got a friend," Eric said. "I have to take him."

Reid looked around. "I don't see anybody."

"I'll get him. It won't take a minute." Eric ran to the brush, untied Gus's chain, and led him out.

Reid was inspecting a front tire by the light of a match when Eric said behind him, "We're ready."

Reid turned around and looked straight into the broad, furry face of Gus. "Yeow!" he bawled. He dropped the match, dived into the truck, and slammed the door. "You said a friend," he yelled out the window.

"Gus is my friend."

"Him! Who're you kidding?"

"But he is." Eric patted Gus between the eyes. He took a piece of hard candy from his pocket and gave it to Gus. Gus chomped on it, smacking his lips and pushing at Eric's hands for more. "See," Eric said.

"I don't believe it!" Reid said. "What the devil are you doing with a brute like that? What goes with you, kid?"

"If you'll let me put him in the back end, I'll explain as we go," Eric said. "You can get out. Gus won't do anything. You'll see."

"By the time I see I could be dead," Reid muttered. But he opened the door carefully and eased to the ground. "I must be nuts to do this. You be sure and hold him. Hear?"

"Don't worry. Gus is tame. You'll see."

"Who's worrying?" Reid opened the back doors and stepped away from the truck. "You put him in. I'm not helpin'."

Eric said, "Get in, Gus. Go on."

Gus just looked at Eric. Eric crawled into the truck, held out a piece of candy, and said, "Come on, if you want it." Gus heaved himself into the truck for the candy. Eric gave it to him, jumped to the ground, and closed the doors.

"Suppose he don't like it in there," Reid worried. "He could rip the truck apart. It's not much but it's all I've got."

"He won't," Eric said. "You'll see."

"Stop saying that. It makes me nervous."

They got into the cab and Reid sat there shaking his head.

"Is anything wrong?" Eric asked.

"He asks, is anything wrong?" Reid was talking to himself. "Here's a kid running around the country with a bear half as big as an elephant and nonchalant as a boy with his dog. And he don't see a thing strange about it!" He looked at Eric soberly. "Kid, one of us is nuts. Oh, not you. Me! For goin' along with this. But I always was a sucker. Maybe I'm doin' this because I don't believe what I saw crawlin' in the back end of this truck. Anyway, here we go. I hope your friend don't mind ridin' in a truck."

"He loves it," Eric said.

They pulled out on the highway and Reid worked up through the gears. Finally he said, "I can't take you all the way. I've got to turn off in about forty miles and go over to the coast for a load. We'll meet a gyppo friend of mine at the Tops Diner. He'll take you right into Portland if he hasn't got a full load, and he usually hasn't. Now, you were gonna tell me how come you're wanderin' around out here with a bear like this. What kind is he, anyhow? I've seen bears, but not like this."

"He's a Kodiak." As Jim Reid drove, Eric told him about Gus and Alaska and the circus.

There was a square opening in the cab between them so the driver could look back to check his load. Eric could hear Gus moving about inspecting the dark interior.

Reid shook his head in amazement when Eric finished. "You sure have had a lot happen to you. You really think you'll make it to Portland and find this fisherman and that he'll take you north?"

Reid concentrated on his driving. "You might, at that. You just might. It's the darndest thing I've ever heard. If I didn't have that bruiser scratching around back there, I wouldn't believe it. A boy and a bear like that hiking across the country. Man, what next!"

Gus suddenly thrust his big head through the opening between them and looked about.

Reid yelled. The truck wobbled crazily. Reid jammed on the brakes with a screech of rubber and yanked open the door to jump.

"It's all right." Eric patted Gus's head. "He just wants to see where we're going."

"You're sure?" Reid took his foot off the brake, but he held the door open.

"Of course. You can see." Eric dug a piece of candy from his pocket and gave it to Gus.

Gus chomped away on the candy, his big black nose twitching as it sucked in all the stray smells in the cab, his little pig eyes under the heavy shelf of forehead bone looking about curiously.

Reid closed the door, but stayed pressed against the side of the cab.

"You can relax," Eric said.

"You can say that!" Reid answered. "But I've never had anything like this in the cab with me before."

Gus continued to look about as the truck sped down the road. He twisted his head and sniffed loudly at Jim Reid. Reid leaned against the door steering with one hand. "Hey! What's he doin' now?"

"Just getting acquainted," Eric explained. "He trusts his nose more than his eyes."

After a few minutes Reid relaxed. He kept glancing at Gus. Finally he began to smile. "Who'd believe it," he said. "Here we are breezin' right down the expressway with the biggest bear in the world practically in the cab with us. How about that? Say, is it okay if I pet him?"

"Lots of people do," Eric said.

Reid reached out a hand gingerly and patted Gus on the head. "You're always feeding him chunks of candy."

"He loves sweets. You want to feed him a piece?"

"Do I get my hand back?"

"Of course." Eric handed him a piece of candy. "Hold it in your palm."

Gus lifted it deftly and Reid laughed delightedly. "I didn't even feel his teeth. Son of a gun!" He patted Gus's head again. "Gus, you're quite a boy! Dave Ford'll never believe this. If I was driving one of them big rigs with him, this'd never happen. Wish I had a camera so I could prove it."

A half hour later they pulled into the parking lot of the Tops Diner. The diner sat at a crossroads and Reid explained that he would turn off here for the coast. There were several trucks in the parking lot and half a dozen cars. Reid glanced about. "He's not here and he should be. I'll check, they know him here." He got out and went into the diner. He returned in a minute. "He's already gone through. It's the first time he's been ahead of me in weeks. He must have made good connections on his pickups. We'll wait a little. There should be another gyppo along soon."

"I wish you were going all the way," Eric said.

"So do I." Reid patted Gus's head. "I feel a personal interest in you and old Gus now. I want to be sure you make it because the odds are so darned big against you. I always pull for the underdog. And, boy, you're way under."

"We could wait someplace until you come back," Eric said, "I'd rather go with you."

"There's no place to wait and I won't be along this way until sometime day after tomorrow. We'll find somebody to take you and Gus in."

They settled down to wait. Now that the truck had stopped, Gus lost interest. He withdrew his head and lay down on the floor.

A big truck and trailer rig rolled in. About ten minutes went by, then an old truck pulled in near them and stopped.

"There's a gyppo." Jim Reid got out of the cab. "Wait here."

The other driver was short, bandy-legged, and very wide through the chest and shoulders. Eric could not hear their voices, but the short driver looked sharply at Reid's truck and began shaking his head. Reid kept talking and the little driver kept shaking his head. Finally he stopped and the two of them came to Reid's truck. The little man climbed into the cab, lit a match, and held it through the opening to look in at Gus. He doused the match, got out, and said, "You didn't exaggerate when you said he was big!"

Jim Reid said, "Eric, this is Ed Bagley. He'll take you and Gus." To Bagley, he said. "Back your truck around so your rear's up against mine and we can transfer the bear easy."

While Bagley was backing around, Reid said, "I had to tell him all about you and Gus going north. He wants ten bucks to take you through the city to Marine Drive. You got any money? If you haven't, maybe I can spare a ten."

Eric pulled out his roll of bills and handed Reid ten dollars.

"Keep that wad out of sight," Reid said. "Don't show it to anyone. Understand? I'll let him think this is my ten."

"All right," Eric said.

It took but a minute to transfer Gus to the other truck and close the door on him. There wasn't as much room for Gus. Bagley had half a truckload of canned goods.

Jim Reid shook hands with Eric and punched his shoulder. "You're less than fifty miles from Portland, Tiger," he said to Eric. "Good luck to you and old Gus. I'll keep my fingers crossed for you all the way." He said to Ed Bagley, "You be sure and deliver 'em to Marine Drive."

"I'll deliver 'em," the driver said.

Jim Reid lifted a hand in farewell and drove off into the night.

# - 13 -

THE TAIL LIGHTS of Jim Reid's truck blended into the highway traffic.

Ed Bagley asked, "You hungry, kid?"

"I could eat something," Eric said.

"How about your friend, what's his name, Gloomy Gus? When do you feed him?"

"He's had enough for today," Eric said.

"Then let's eat."

Eric had a piece of pie and a glass of milk. Bagley had coffee, a sandwich, and pie. After he'd finished he sat, elbows on the counter, and smoked a cigarette. His eyes narrowed thoughtfully. From time to time he squinted through the smoke at Eric. Finally he tamped out the cigarette and said, "Well, let's ramble."

Eric carefully extracted coins from his pocket without pulling out the bills and paid for his milk and pie.

The truck was older and noisier than Jim Reid's. The body creaked and worked. The cab was drafty.

Bagley said, "Guess you're havin' plenty of trouble gettin' to Portland, especially since you're hitchin' with a bear."

"Yes," Eric said.

"He's really one of them big ones? Whatta they call them big Alaskan bears?"

"Kodiak. Yes."

"Saw a circus ad in a store window a couple of months ago. It musta been about your bear. Said he was the biggest bear on earth, or somethin' like that, and that he was the only tame Kodiak in the world. That so?"

"He's the only tame one," Eric said. "I don't know if he's the biggest."

They drove a few minutes in silence. The old truck gradually picked up speed. Bagley asked, "How come you're runnin' off from the circus. Don't it pay good?"

"I'm going home."

"That right?" Bagley nodded. "Reid did say you lived in Alaska. You're a long ways from home. You got folks down here?"

"No," Eric said.

The old truck began laboring up a grade and Bagley was busy shifting gears. Then, "That circus must be wonderin' where you and the bear are about now. Bet they'd sure be surprised if they knew you was in a truck and headed for Portland."

"I suppose so."

"Bear like that must be worth lotsa money — bein' the only tame one in the world and all. I bet most any circus would be glad to get him."

Eric only nodded. He was not as comfortable with Bagley as he'd been with Reid. This probing talk made him nervous.

The truck came out on top of the grade. The road tipped down and they began a long gradual descent through a corridor of big timber. They picked up speed and rattled along at a rapid clip.

Ed Bagley rambled on about Gus. "They sure did advertise that bear. I saw signs lotsa places, even in the paper, and heard it on the radio. Costs lots to advertise. They musta made a lotta money showin' him around."

"I don't know," Eric said.

"Sure you do. They had big crowds, didn't they?"

"There were a lot of other acts and trained animals besides Gus."

"But it was him they advertised most," Bagley pointed

out. "So it was the bear that made 'em the money."

"It could be," Eric agreed. He didn't like Bagley and the way this talk was going. He'd be glad when they were out of the truck. "How long will it take to get to Portland?" he asked, trying to get the man's mind on something else.

"Couple of short hours. Maybe a little less."

"Do you know where Marine Drive is?"

"I know that town like the palm of my hand."

They came out on the bottom of the grade and began running on the level. "Yes, sir, I bet that circus would pay plenty to get this bear back."

"Money doesn't matter," Eric said. "We're going home."

"Oh, sure. Still and all..." Bagley lapsed into thoughtful silence.

Eric glanced at him sharply and said nothing.

They rattled on for a few minutes. Then Bagley observed almost to himself, "Bet there'll be quite a reward out for you and this bear."

Gus began scratching at the floor and rattling his chain. Eric knew he was turning around to lie down. But he said to Bagley, "The first time we get to one of those highway rest stops we'd better pull in and give the bear a drink."

"Let him wait. We'll be in the city in a little while."

"He's not used to waiting. He drinks a lot of water," Eric explained. "If you don't want the inside of this truck torn up, you'd better stop."

"I got nothin' to put water in. You're sure he won't wait?"

"I know Gus. When we stop I'll find something."

"There's a stop up ahead three or four miles."

A few minutes later they came to a narrow road that led off the highway into a grove of trees. Bagley stopped at a faucet that rose from a concrete slab.

Eric climbed out and went around to the back.

Bagley got out of the cab but didn't come near. "I ain't helpin'," he said. "I'm not goin' near that bear."

"I don't need help."

"There's no bucket. What're you gonna give him a drink in?"

"There's a depression under that faucet," Eric said. "He can drink from that." Eric opened the doors and Gus stood looking down at him. He grasped the chain and pulled. "Come on, Gus. Come on."

Gus came down out of the truck and stood swinging his head, nose sampling the night breezes. Eric grasped the chain close to his neck and led him off a few feet. Then he turned and faced Bagley. "You can close those doors and take off. This is as far as we're going with you."

"W-h-a-t! Are you crazy? I thought you wanted to get to Portland?"

"We'll get there."

"Not without me and my truck. What's the matter with you, kid?"

"There's nothing wrong with me," Eric held tight to Gus. "We're not going any farther with you. You go on. We'll make out."

"How?"

"You needn't worry. We'll do it."

"You're really dumb. The first person that sees you and that bear will call the cops," Bagley pointed out. "Then you'll be right back in that circus you're runnin' away from."

"I figure that first person might be you," Eric said.

"Me! Why'd I do a thing like that?"

"For a reward maybe."

Bagley shook his head in amazement. "Kids get the darndest notions. Whatever gave you that idea?"

"You talk too much."

"I was tryin' to be friendly."

"Maybe," Eric said.

"You're makin' a big mistake."

"It's my mistake."

"Man, are you a stubborn kid," Bagley said annoyed. "I'm not about to stand here and argue with you all night. I agreed to take you to Marine Drive. I figure to do that." He started forward purposefully.

Eric took hold of the snap on the chain. "I'll turn Gus loose," he warned.

Bagley pulled up and looked at Gus. Eric twitched the chain slightly. Gus lifted his big head and stared at Bagley. The man began backing away. "Okay," he said angrily, "it's your funeral."

"That's right." Eric watched the old truck rattle off onto the highway.

Eric led Gus away from the rest stop into the dark under the trees. They stumbled about for some time, then came into a dirt trail and followed it. The trail fed into an old, abandoned, paved road almost overgrown with brush. They went steadily down the road away from the superhighway. The traffic noises gradually faded. The silence and the dark were mysteriously eerie, and Eric reached a hand to Gus's neck for reassurance. "I sure am glad you're with me," he said. Gus padded unconcernedly along, big feet making sandpapery whispers on the old roadway. The road ended abruptly at the lip of a ravine. Eric stopped uncertainly. A half-moon sailed from behind a bank of clouds and bathed the earth faintly. To the right Eric made out open fields. He turned that way. The fields were long grass and low brush. He was soon soaked to the waist by the heavy dew. Gus shook himself, spraying water over Eric. They plodded on.

Once across the fields the land tilted down. Far off through the moon's pale shine Eric made out the black bulk of big trees again. A breeze poured up the hill, cool and damp and heavy with the scent of ferns and decaying wood. A night-prowling animal passed furtively through the grass ahead of them and vanished. Gus gave an explosive "Whoof." Eric patted him and said again, "I sure am glad you're along." The moon sailed behind the clouds and the earth was frighteningly dark and still. Lights of a house burned far ahead of them. The probing headlights of a car wound into the black density of the distant trees.

Eric was chilled and his teeth were chattering when they

148

finally entered the fringe of trees. It was very dark and the fir needles were soft underfoot. But the brush was gone and the hiking was easy. He came out on a narrow gravel road and followed it. In a cleared space he came to a small country store. Beyond the store the massive blackness of the trees closed down again. The road tipped steeply and they walked between huge, still columns of fir. Eric stopped once, uncertain and a little fearful. Gus thrust up his big nose. Eric put an arm around his huge neck and felt reassured. He went forward walking close beside Gus finding courage and confidence in the bear's great body, the nonchalant manner with which he paced into this unknown dark.

The road wound about and Eric had the feeling they were approaching something. A few minutes later they came to a small river making a crooked streak between low, brushy banks. The road stopped before a cabin on the creek bank.

Eric studied the dark cabin. There was no sign of life. A car shed was attached to one end. But there was no car. He glanced at Gus to see if he was swinging that delicate nose up to sample some strange scent. But Gus was only interested in a clump of grass.

Eric tied Gus to a tree and inspected the building. He walked around peering into the windows. He saw the vague outlines of furniture, a stove in the kitchen, cupboards with the doors closed, a bedroom with the bare mattress on the bed. Every window and door was locked tight. In the shed he found a rowboat and a pair of oars. This must be a vacation cabin locked up for the winter. He was cold and chilled. If he could just get inside, light a fire, dry his clothes, and get warm. He'd like to sleep on that mattress tonight. But there was no entrance, unless he broke a window. He searched through the shed. He found nothing. FInally he took Gus into the shed and tied him to a center post. Gus settled down to sleep. Eric sat on the floor, his back against the upturned rowboat. He turned up his collar and pulled up his knees. He thought about Jim Reid and Ed Bagley. He wondered where Gus and he were and how much farther it was to the city. How were they going to get there without being seen and picked up by the police? He was too cold and tired to make any decision tonight. He huddled down in his coat, listened to the steady murmur of the river beyond the shed, and fell asleep.

Eric awoke stiff and sore. His clothes clung damply to his body and he was ravenously hungry. Gus was standing at the end of his chain looking out at the bright spring morning, his nose casting for wayward scents.

Once again Eric circled the house and tried the doors and windows hoping he'd missed something in the dark. The only thing he'd missed was a narrow log footbridge spanning the river behind the house. He remembered the little country store he'd passed last night and said to Gus, "You relax. I'm going to get us something to eat," and started up the road.

A small bell tinkled as Eric went through the door. A little bald man wearing glasses and a white apron came from the back. He smiled at Eric and said, "My, you're early, young man. I don't usually get anyone in here before noon and sometimes not then. What can I do for you?"

Eric looked around. The store had only a half-dozen counters and not much of an assortment of groceries. He picked out five loaves of bread and the man said, "That bread's two days old. If you'd like to wait an hour or so, they'll be bringing fresh bread this morning."

"This will be fine," Eric said. He added three heads of limp-looking lettuce, a pound of bologna, and another pound of hard candy.

The little man made change and asked, "I've never seen you around before. Do you live near here?"

"We just stopped for overnight." Eric waved vaguely toward the river.

"You must be staying by the bluff."

"Yes." Eric gathered up his purchases. As he hurried down the road he thought angrily, "Darn! Why didn't I get some matches?"

At the cabin he gave Gus all the bread but eight slices and the three head of lettuce. He made two sandwiches for himself out of half the bologna, wrapped the four remaining slices of bread and bologna in one of the bread wrappers and laid it on a shelf for a later meal. Then, his stomach full, he sat down to plan how they'd get to Portland and Marine Drive. They had to go in some sort of covered truck. That meant a gyppo. Where would he get one and how would he be sure he wasn't getting another Ed Bagley? There was no way. He could do just one thing; stay here tonight. Early in the morning he'd find the expressway and intercept Jim Reid as he headed for Portland. That decided, he took Gus across the footbridge and tied him to a tree in a small meadow of deep grass. "Get a good feed to go with that bread and lettuce," he said. "It's all you're going to get today."

The day was getting warm for spring. A small breeze rattled the new leaves and bent the grass blades. The river sparkled like silver under the sun. The bridge surface had dried and Eric stretched out on his stomach to let the heat soak into him. He looked idly down into the water and tried to imagine it was Friday Creek.

When he awoke, it was well past noon and he was hungry again. He glanced over at Gus and could just see his big body lying in the deep grass. His stomach full, he was taking a nap. Eric returned to the shed, made himself a sandwich, and sat on the upturned boat while he ate. He had just finished when he heard tires on the gravel road to the cabin. He jumped up, started to run outside, then realized it was too late. He rushed around the boat, flopped on his stomach behind it, and lay still.

Eric peeked around the bow and saw a state-police car stop before the cabin. A trooper with the little bald store owner got out. The trooper tried the back door, and the little store owner said, "Like I told you, he came in early this morning before I was hardly open. His clothes looked like they'd been slept in and they were kind of wet, you know. He bought five loaves of bread, a pound of bologna, three old heads of lettuce I was going to throw out today, and a pound of hard candy. That's enough bread to feed a dozen big men, but not enough bologna for more than just about three. And nobody'd want that lettuce. Well, it just looked suspicious so I asked him where he was staying and he waved down by the river. I said, you must be staying by the bluff then, and he said 'yes.' Now you know there ain't a bluff for twenty miles. That's why I called you."

"You say you never saw him before?" the officer asked, peering through a window.

"Nope. I tell you there was something mighty funny about that kid. Somebody broke into this cabin last fall and lived here about a week near as John Moore could tell. Told Moore I'd look out for it this winter. You figure a gang could have holed up in it again?"

"No telling," the officer said. "Is there another door?"

"Around the other side."

Both men disappeared and Eric was tempted to jump up and run outside. But they might reappear any second, so he hugged the floor close to the side of the boat and waited.

A minute later the men reappeared. The officer was saying, "There's nothing amiss. I don't see any sign..." His voice trailed off. Eric heard feet enter the shed and held his breath. When next the officer spoke, he was on the other side of the boat. "Here's four bread wrappers. And here's another on the shelf with a couple of slices of bread and a piece of bologna." The feet came toward the boat again.

The little grocer's voice said, "Here's a couple of lettuce leaves."

The feet turned and left the shed.

The officer's voice said, "Your hunch was right. Somebody was here, but there's nothing to indicate how many. It's an odd order all right, five loaves of bread and that other stuff. Anyway, whoever they are did no damage and they seem to be gone. But I'll keep an eye on the cabin from now on."

They got into the police car and drove away.

Eric rose from behind the boat. They had taken the bread wrappers from the floor and the one on the shelf that held the two slices of bread and bologna. He knew immediately they could not stay here tonight. The officer would be returning to check on the place. He and Gus had to leave.

Eric crossed the bridge and found Gus had excavated a hole some three feet deep in search of something he meant to eat. He coaxed Gus out with a couple of pieces of candy, unfastened the chain from the tree, and led him away. He hesitated, getting his directions straight, then cut off through the timber heading back for the superhighway.

The sun was dropping behind a distant line of mountains when they came out of screening brush on the brow of a low hill. They looked down on the racing traffic of the four-lane road. A long, straight stretch was visible to the south. Just what Eric needed to spot Reid in time to flag him down.

A short distance off was a big fir tree whose thick branches had kept the carpet of fir needles dry. It was a good place to spend the night. He fastened Gus to the tree and gave him a couple of pieces of hard candy, and the bear flopped down prepared to take a nap. "You're lucky," Eric said. "You've got practically five loaves of bread, three heads of lettuce, and a lot of grass and roots inside you. I'm hungry. I wish I had that bologna and those slices of bread the officer took."

Eric sat under the fir tree and watched the highway below. Night closed down. The lights from passing cars hit the four lanes at intervals. A pale half-moon glinted on the new leaves of maple, willow and hazel. A keen wind blew against him. Eric turned up the collar of his jacket and moved around the bowl of the tree to get in the lee of the wind. He dozed and awoke and dozed again. Gus moved only once. He rose, turned around several times, and lay down again. The wind ruffled his thick coat but he slept peacefully without moving again.

With the coming of dawn Eric led Gus back to a cleared place where the grass was thick and tied the chain to a rock. He gave him a couple of pieces of candy, patted his head reassuringly, and scratched his ears until he rumbled deep in his chest. Then he returned to watch the highway.

The traffic thickened. At times both northbound lanes

were almost a solid stream of cars and trucks. Eric moved down closer to the highway. The morning hours slipped away. The sun rose, bringing spring warmth heavy with the odor of bursting buds and new growth. A swarm of canaries flitted through the brush, then fled across the highway above the traffic, going north. A pair of doves landed nearby and Eric was surprised to hear their murmuring above the traffic noise. The first robin he'd seen this spring pecked at a bud near him. It was frightened away by the sudden blast of a truck horn.

Eric watched all morning for the old red truck with REID painted on the front and sides. At noon he ran up and moved Gus to a new spot of fresh grass, gave him a couple of pieces of candy, and returned to the highway.

He was getting terribly hungry. He checked the candy and found he had about half a pound left. He allowed himself two pieces and they cut the sharp edge of his appetite.

The afternoon dragged. His eyes began to burn from steady watching. He was almost afraid to blink for fear he might miss the truck. His hunger sharpened again and he ate another piece of candy. A half-dozen times he was sure the truck was coming but it always turned out to be some other. He ran up and moved Gus again.

The sun dropped toward the distant ragged mountains and he began to worry. Had the truck gone by in the dark of early morning? Had it passed during the few minutes he'd gone to move Gus? Had it somehow gone by right under his eyes?

The sun dropped out of the sky. Shadows chased across the valley. The warmth of the day was gone. Headlights began to show in the passing traffic stream. Darkness came and the wind had a bite. Finally the traffic was no more than streaking black blobs behind headlights. He knew with a sick feeling he was not going to find Jim Reid. Either he had missed Reid or the truck had gone another direction.

Eric returned to Gus. The bear had eaten the grass down as far as the short chain would permit. He pushed at Eric's hands searching for something sweet. Eric searched his pockets and discovered he had only two pieces of candy left. He'd eaten the rest during the afternoon and evening. He gave Gus one and ate the other. He moved Gus again and sat down against the rock to think. Doubts poured in upon him. They would never reach the city. It was impossible to stay hidden much longer. They needed food. He hadn't realized until this moment what an impossibly crazy thing he was trying to do. Charlie had tried to tell him. Charlie had said something else, too. "With luck and a lot of fight, crazy ideas sometimes work out. You just might make it."

Gus sat on his haunches, stretched his nose, and sniffed hopefully. Eric patted his head and said, "We had our luck, didn't we? We got away from the circus. We met Jim Reid. We got away from Ed Bagley. The police didn't catch us back at the cabin. We're about forty miles from Marine Drive and Pete Clark. Luck got us this far." He felt his confidence and determination returning. Now he had to think and plan every move. No more trusting to luck, no more taking chances. "From here on," he said to Gus, "the fighting part begins."

# - 14 -

ERIC WAS AWAKE when the first dawn chased the night shadows. He was stiff and cold, but by swinging his arms and stomping his feet he soon restored circulation. Gus had been busy for some time. He had excavated a hole at the base of a nearby bush and found something he was eating. "You're lucky," Eric said, unfastening the chain from the tree. "I'm almost starved."

They hiked off across an open, deep-grassed field. The night's dew clung in thick drops to the grass blades, and soon Eric was wet to the knees. Far in the distance he could see the ragged, black pattern of a mountain range. He knew that between them and that range lay the broad floor of a large valley. He had learned in touring with the circus that these valley floors held rich soil and were intensively farmed. He'd seen trucks standing about most farms. He would stop at the most likely looking and offer the eighty-odd dollars he had left for their transportation to Portland.

Morning light spread across the farm mountain ridges and moved in formless waves out over the valley floor. The sky turned blue. The sun sailed into view and Eric felt its first faint warmth.

Eric and Gus stood on a ridge and the valley lay spread out in green checkerboards of grain fields, orchards, and pastures. Several miles away he could see the narrow ribbon of a market road. Farm buildings and homes fronted on the road. The road was empty this early and there was no movement around the farm buildings. He worked down the slope toward the nearest cluster of buildings and studied them. The house was big and there were many large outbuildings. Behind the huge barn a field was filled with grazing cattle. The place did not look inviting.

They travelled parallel but well above the road, crossing fields and brush patches as they made their way toward the next farm. The sun climbed and dried the grass blades. An occasional car or farm truck passed on the road below. He began to see tractors working in fields. He tired and stopped to rest. He was ravenously hungry and he knew Gus was, too. It was getting hard to manage Gus. He continually wanted to investigate grass clumps or old rotting logs. A squirrel sat on a rock in front of them and chattered angrily, then popped into a hole beside the rock. Gus wanted to dig it out and Eric had trouble getting him to go on. They crossed a small creek and Gus stopped to drink. Eric didn't know how pure the water was, but he lay on his stomach and filled up. It helped ease the hunger pangs. They found a marshy spot dotted with skunk-cabbage plants and Gus insisted on eating them all before going on.

The farms they passed continued to look imposing. The sun climbed past the zenith and began tipping toward the western hills. The day was warm for this time of year and Eric opened his jacket. The hunger pangs began again and that fine confidence of morning was deserting him. The valley took a gradual turn to the left, then straightened out again. Eric found himself looking almost directly down onto the roofs of farm buildings beneath him. The house was small, neat, and white with a lawn in front. There was washing hanging on the line behind the house. The few outbuildings looked in good repair. Behind the barn a dozen cows grazed in a field. Beyond that was an orchard in full leaf. Far back there, a man was repairing a fence.

Eric's eyes returned to the clothesline as a woman came out of the back of the house carrying a basket. She began taking clothes from the basket and hanging them on the line. Eric watched until the woman finished and returned to the house. Then he said to Gus, "That's where we're going. We're going to talk to those people. Come on."

They worked their way down through the thin scattering of brush and trees almost to the road. From the last fringe of trees they stopped, and Eric studied the house and outbuildings again. Close up it looked even more inviting and homelike. He tied Gus to a tree, well out of sight from the road, patted his head and said, "You relax. I'll be back soon," and crossed the road. He noticed the name on the mailbox — FRED ROBBINS.

The woman that answered the door was rather short and stout. She had a mass of gray-streaked hair and a smiling, friendly face.

Eric stood there. The fine things he'd planned to say, the businesslike approach to buy help for Gus and himself, were gone. The happenings of the past days, the uncertainties, his hunger and tiredness, and the immensity of what he was trying to do robbed him of words.

The woman smiled and said, "Well, how do you do?" When he said nothing, she continued, "I haven't seen you before. You're new around here, aren't you?"

Eric nodded. He swallowed desperately to clear his throat.

"Is there something I can do for you?" she asked.

He found his voice then. But the words were not sure and confident as they should have been. "I've got to have help. I tried so hard. I can't go any farther alone."

She studied him a moment, then drew him through the door into a living room and pushed him into a chair. She sat opposite and folded her hands. "Now," she smiled, "who are you and what is it you want help with?"

"I'm Eric," he said. "Gus and I want to go home."

She probed gently. "What's your last name, Eric?"

For the first time it came to Eric that his name was not Strong. He shook his head. "I don't know."

She studied him a moment. "Where is home and who is

Gus?"

"Tatouche, Alaska." He drew a deep breath and said in a careful voice, "Gus is a bear."

"A what!" She smiled uncertainly. "I thought you said bear."

"I left him across the road in the brush."

Mrs. Robbins sat very still. "You did say 'bear,' didn't you? Yes, of course you did. I heard you." For a moment she seemed confused. Then she said, "Let's start over, shall we? You don't know your last name. You're going home — to Alaska. You've got a — a bear out there in the brush." She waved her arm vaguely. "And you need help. Whew! You'd better take it from there."

"You want to hear it all?"

"Don't you think I should?"

Eric began to talk. Under the woman's smiling encouragement he told the story of Gus, Ten-Day Watson, Ned Strong and the circus. When he finished, she was shaking her head in wonder. "I can't believe it! I just can't believe it. But no one could make up such a tale. And you say your bear, this Gus, is right across the road in the brush tied to a tree?"

Eric nodded, "Yes, ma'am."

She jumped up. "Fred's got to hear this. Sit right there. Don't move!" She left the room and Eric heard a bell ringing on the back porch. She returned and sat opposite him. "And now you need help getting into Portland so the bear won't be seen," she said.

"If I can just get to Marine Drive where Pete Clark lives. He promised to take us back to Alaska in his boat. I'll pay for taking us in."

The back door opened and a man walked into the room. "What's the bell for, Norah?" He was big, with a shock of blond hair and the heavy shoulders and chest of a man who'd worked hard.

The woman said, "Fred, this is Eric. I want you to sit down and listen to him. You won't believe what he says, but listen."

159

The man smiled at Eric, then scowled at the woman. "What goes on? What's the big mystery? I got work to do."

"I know you have," Norah Robinson said, "but just sit down and listen, Fred. Eric, tell him everything you told me."

When Eric finished, he asked, "How old are you, son?"

"Almost fifteen."

Robbins glanced at his wife. "Already he's lived more than I have. You say this bear of yours is right across the road in the brush? Bring him over and I'll believe this crazy story."

Eric returned to Gus. He had eaten the grass around the tree and was digging for roots. Eric untied him and said, "Come on. Maybe we've found some help."

He led Gus around to the back of the house where the man and woman stood on the porch. The woman gasped, "Oh, good heavens!" and backed up to the open door. The man came warily off the porch and walked all around Gus at a safe distance.

"Man, oh man!" Fred Robbins kept saying. "What a bruiser! What a bruiser! I've hunted all my life, but never been North. I've read about these fellows and seen pictures, but I've never seen one. I knew they were big, but not this big."

"Will you take us to Portland, to Marine Drive?" Eric asked. "I don't mean for nothing." He pulled the roll of bills from his pocket. "I can pay."

"Where'd you get that?"

"I earned it with our act in the circus."

"You're sure you didn't steal it?"

"Fred!" Mrs. Robbins said, shocked. "What a thing to say."

"Look, Norah, this boy comes in here out of nowhere leading an animal like this, his pocket full of money, and with a tale as wild as you'll ever hear. It's got to be questioned. We could get in real trouble if he's stolen that money."

"I didn't," Eric insisted.

"Oh, don't be so suspicious," Mrs. Robbins said, annoyed.

"One of us has to be." Robbins looked at Eric. "I'd like to

believe you, boy. But by your own admission you are running away."

"From a no-good that passed himself off as his father and a circus man that wants to use him."

"That could be a mighty convenient story."

"But it isn't." Mrs. Robbins smiled at her husband. "You don't really think so either, do you?"

Fred Robbins fidgeted uncomfortably. "It's just wild enough to be true," he admitted. "But I can't just pick up and run off when the notion strikes me. I've got spring work to do. That big field needs disking and it'll be time to milk in another three hours."

"You said this morning that field was too wet to work yet," Mrs. Robbins reminded him. "And Alec Norris said he'd milk for you anytime you called him. Besides, you promised to take me shopping when the spring sales came. They're beginning now."

"It'll be dark by the time we can get to the city. Stores will be closed."

"They're open tonight until nine thirty."

"It would be better if we got in when it's dark," Eric ventured.

"There you are," Mrs. Robbins said. "That settles it."

Fred Robbins shook his head," This is crazy, Norah."

"People should be a little crazy once in a while."

"But this is going overboard."

"What else can we do? Tell this boy and his pet to go on, we can't be bothered? Then try to forget he was ever here?"

Fred Robbins scowled and scuffed his toe in the dirt. "All right," he said finally. "But we don't have a closed truck, only a pickup with a stock rack. It'll hold two cows. It ought to hold one bear. I'll have to wrap canvas around the slatted sides so no one can see inside and we'll have to chain him short to the floor so he can't go out over the top."

"That's more like my Fred." Mrs. Robbins smiled at Eric. "We'll take you and your Gus to Portland and it won't cost a cent."

Gus kept swinging his big head and wrinkling his black nose. He whoofed suddenly and Mrs. Robbins jumped.

"Why does he keep doing that?" she asked nervously.

"He's hungry," Eric said. "He smells food."

"Of course," she said. "You must be hungry, too. When did you eat last?"

"Yesterday morning."

"Oh, my! A boy your age! Fred, you and Eric put Gus in the barn, then come right up to the house. I'll get something to eat. And we'll have to feed Gus. What does he eat?"

"Most anything," Eric said. "He likes all kinds of fruit, apples, pears, and the like, and vegetables. We usually give him three or four heads of lettuce a day and four or five loaves of bread. He likes any kind of sweets."

"No raw meat?"

"Bears aren't much for meat, except salmon. Gus eats lots of salmon during the big runs in Alaska. His special treat at home is pancakes with syrup."

"Pancakes with syrup coming up," Mrs. Robbins smiled. "We'll see what we can do about a couple of loaves of bread. There's some old doughnuts from last week."

"We've got the last of our winter apples and cabbage and carrots in the cool room," Fred Robbins added. "They're getting a little shriveled and the cabbage is kind of soft, but it's good yet. We'll make out. Let's take him to the barn."

They tied Gus to a center post and Fred Robbins gave him half a box of apples, four heads of winter cabbage, and a dozen big carrots. "That should hold him until we get back with some doughnuts and pancakes."

In the kitchen Mrs. Robbins had a pitcher of milk, cereal, eggs, and toast for Eric. She had pancakes on the griddle. "You can have some, too," she said. "But these are for Gus. Can he eat a dozen big ones along with everything else?"

"Easy," Eric said.

"Then a dozen it'll be. Sit down and dig in, Eric. Fred, if the pickup's ready you better change clothes."

"It's ready. I won't drape the canvas around the sides

until we put the bear inside."

Eric ate until he could eat no more, then Fred Robbins backed the pickup down to the barn to load Gus.

Eric untied the chain and held out a pancake. Gus relished it with a great smacking of lips. "That's the first pancake you've had since we left Tatouche," Eric said. He gave Gus another and another. "This is almost like home, huh? We're going to make it all the way in to Pete Clark's now. In another week you'll be having pancakes every morning at Ten-Day Watson's and you can go fishing, too. What do you think of that?"

Gus lifted his nose and sniffed at the boy. Then he reached for another pancake.

Mrs. Robbins smiled delightedly. "Why, that's cute!"

Eric fed Gus all but two of the pancakes, then he jumped into the back of the pickup and held them out for Gus to see. "If you want them, come on in. Come on, Gus." Gus heaved himself into the pickup and Eric dropped the pancakes on the floor and climbed out.

Fred Robbins replaced the tailgate while Eric ran Gus's chain through a ring in the floor and secured it. They draped canvas around the sides of the stock rack and were ready to leave.

"That," Fred Robbins smiled," was as easy as taking candy from a baby, or should I say a bear?"

They breezed down the freeway right into Portland. Gus, his stomach full, stretched out on the truck floor and enjoyed the ride.

By the time they reached Marine Drive full night blackened the river.

"Do you remember the house number, Eric?" Mrs. Robbins asked.

"No, but it was big. I think sixteen something. Pete Clark's name should be on the mailbox, shouldn't it?"

"Probably," Fred Robbins said. "This is eight hundred. We've got a ways to go."

They drove slowly for a mile or more. Eric clenched his

fists so tightly his knuckles hurt. His palms were sweaty and he wiped them on his pants. Finally the headlights picked out the name: P. CLARK, 1620 MARINE DRIVE. "That's it!" Eric's heart jumped into his throat. "That's it! I remember the number now."

Pete Clark's home sat in an area with no other house near. It fronted on the drive and Eric could see the dark flow of the river almost at the back door. There was a light at the back of the house, but the rest was dark.

"It looks dark," Mrs. Robbins observed. "Eric, go make sure someone's home. We'll wait."

Eric left the pickup, climbed the porch step, and pressed the bell. He waited, then pressed it again. No lights came on. There was no sound within. He went around to the back door and knocked. He knocked again and again. He peeked through a window and he could see into the kitchen and part of a hall. The light was in the hall. He carefully tried the door. It was locked.

A boathouse was moored to the bank and he ran down to see if it held the *Lady Lou*. Through the window he made out the dim shape of a boat in the inner dark. It was big enough to be a seiner.

He returned to the house and walked around it. There was a garage on the far side. The doors yawned open and the car was gone. He felt relief. They were out somewhere. He returned to the pickup and said, "The boat's in the boathouse but there's no one home. The garage is open and the car's gone. They've just gone out. They'll be back. Gus and I'll wait."

"Where will you wait?" Mrs. Robbins asked. "You don't want anyone to see Gus."

Eric looked around. About a hundred feet off, part of an old dock jutted into the river. The side facing them was open. "We can wait under that dock until they come home," he said.

"I don't like to leave you here alone," Mrs. Robbins said. "Maybe we'd better wait around to make sure."

"We'll be all right," Eric said. "I know we will."

"You're sure this Pete Clark came right out and said he'd take you north?" Fred Robbins asked.

"Yes. He even gave me the address of his home. But I only remembered the sixteen part."

"Seems like it should be all right, then."

"I don't know," Mrs. Robbins worried.

"This is the place I've been trying to get to." He spread his hands. "And now we're here."

Fred Robbins said, "Well, all right." He got out and removed the tailgate and Gus came down to the road.

Mrs. Robbins said, "Write and let us know how you got home. Box forty-two, Rickreall."

"I will," Eric said. "I'd like to pay you."

Fred Robbins shook hands with him and got back in the pickup. "You hang on to that money. You're not home yet."

"We soon will be," Eric said and watched them drive away.

Eric led Gus into the black dark under the old dock and tied his chain to a piling. Gus snorted and swung his head. Eric guessed he was picking up the clean, fresh smell of the river and maybe remembering Friday Creek. "It won't be long now." He sat down on the sand and leaned against a piling to wait.

At intervals private boats passed with small chuffing sounds. An occasional outboard snarled noisily. Gradually the river traffic ceased. Infrequently cars passed on the road. Several times he heard voices. But Pete Clark's home remained dark. Gus finally stretched out with a sigh, prepared to go to sleep.

The luminous dial on Eric's watch showed almost midnight when a car turned off the road and entered the garage. A moment later lights came on in the house.

Eric returned to the back door and knocked. The woman who answered was tall and thin. Her voice was sharp. "Yes?"

"Is Pete Clark in?" Eric asked.

"Why?"

"He said he'd take Gus and me back north with him

when he went. Our home is in Tatouche, Alaska."

"Not another one!" The woman looked him up and down. "He's picked up some odd ones in the past but never any kids before. Well, he's been gone for a week."

"Gone!" Eric stammered. "But the boat's in the boat-house."

"A friend rents the boathouse while Pete's fishing. That's his boat."

"But Pete said he'd take us…"

"I don't care what he said." The woman was angry. "He's gone. Gone! Can't you understand plain English? He pulled out a week ago. Now you get out of here, boy. Go on, beat it." She slammed the door.

Eric went down the steps, crossed to the old dock, and went underneath. He sat down beside Gus. Gus poked his nose at his hands and whoofed, searching for sweets. Eric patted his head absently. Pete Clark gone! All his scheming and fighting to get here had been for nothing. Under this old dock on the bank of the Columbia River two thousand miles from home his trail had ended.

He was still sitting there when a car stopped before Pete Clark's home. A red light kept flashing from the top of the car. He heard the woman's voice saying, "He was a young fellow, maybe fourteen or fifteen. I couldn't be sure on that dark back porch. But I watched him go under the open end of the old dock. There's two of them. He said the other's name was Gus. I don't want strangers hanging around here in the middle of the night."

Two men came toward the open end of the dock. The woman followed behind. Eric jumped up and looked wildly about for someplace to hide or run to. The powerful beam of a flashlight stabbed under the dock and pinned him in its glare. A commanding voice said, "All right, fellow, come out of there! This is the police."

# - 15 -

ERIC FUMBLED at the chain, unfastening Gus. The woman let out a frightened gasp, ran for the house, and slammed the door. One of the officers said sharply, "Just a minute, boy. What've you got there?"

"This is Gus," Eric said.

"Gus!" the smaller of the two officers said. "It looks an awful lot like a bear to me. Don't untie that thing, boy! Don't untie him!"

Eric could see the shine of guns in the officers' hands. He said in a frantic rush, "You don't have to worry. He's tame. He's a circus bear." He put an arm around Gus's neck and Gus lifted his big nose and sniffed at the boy. "Please put those guns away," Eric begged. "He won't hurt anybody."

"Not as long as he stays tied and we keep out of range," the tall officer said. "You keep him tied. Hear?"

"He is tied,"Eric said.

"Good. Now come out here and tell us all about this. Man, I've dealt with some things in thirty years on the force. We've tended chickens and ducks, dogs and cats, even cows and a prize bull that got loose once. Even had to round up skunks and a boa constrictor. But a bear and a kid? Let's have it boy, from the beginning."

"Gus and I are from Alaska. We joined the Marcel and Son Circus last fall," Eric said. He told it in a rush, right down to tonight.

When he stopped, the tall officer said, "You mean to tell

me, you and that bear have come all the way from Fir Crest to Marine Drive without being picked up or even seen by a patrol car? Come off it, boy! I've got a kid about your age and if he came up with a whopper like that I'd tan his hide."

"It's true," Eric insisted.

"It doesn't make much sense."

The smaller officer asked, "What kind of bear is he?"

"He's a Kodiak," Eric said.

"You mean one of them big Alaskan bears?"

"He's the only tame one in the world," Eric said. "The circus says he's the biggest."

"I can believe that," the smaller officer said. "You say he's tame?"

"You can see he's with me. You can pet him."

"Thanks. I'll take your word for it."

The tall officer said, "Ed, get on the radio and tell them what we've got here."

"What're you going to do with us?" Eric asked fearfully.

The tall officer shook his head. "I don't make that decision."

Eric could hear the radio conversation Ed was having. "We've got a young kid out here with a tame bear."

"That's funny," the radio voice said, "I could have sworn you said bear. Talk plainer."

"I said bear — b-e-a-r."

"A bear! Where'd a bear come from? I'll send down a man with a rifle."

"This is a trained bear. A circus bear."

"Oh, well. Bring him and the kid in."

"Not in this prowl car."

"Oh, come off it! Those circus bears aren't so big. You've got room."

"Did you ever see a big bear?"

"Sure. He weighed five hundred pounds."

"This one will make more than two of that five-hundred pounder."

"Blacks don't get that big."

168

"Who said he's a black bear? This is an Alaskan Kodiak. Send the paddy."

"You've got to be kidding!"

"Sure I am. Send the paddy wagon."

"Paddy coming up," the voice said, "and one rifle."

Eric said, "He's tame. You're not going to shoot him?"

"It's just a precaution," the big officer said. "There's nothing to worry about."

The paddy looked like a closed panel truck with double doors in the rear. There were two officers in the front seat. One held a rifle. They backed the paddy wagon as close to the old dock as possible and opened the back doors. "Now, son," the tall officer said, "can you bring that animal out and put him in there?"

"Yes, sir," Eric said. "You aren't going to hurt him?"

"We don't want to. We'll leave you a clear path to the paddy wagon. You take 'em in and we'll close the doors."

Eric went under the dock, untied Gus, and said, "Come on. We're going for another ride." Gus sniffed and pushed at his hands, and Eric said, "No more candy. I'm all out." He led Gus from under the dock.

The officer with the rifle backed a startled step and jerked up the rifle. The second policeman breathed, "Oh, man!"

The tall officer said, "Maybe the doors aren't high enough."

Eric led Gus up to the paddy wagon and went in first. Gus hesitated. Eric pulled on the chain and held out his hand. "Come on, Gus," he said. "Come on." Gus put his paws on the top step, then heaved himself inside. His back scraped the top of the door opening. Eric said to the tall officer, "You can close the doors now."

"You're going to ride in there with him?" the driver asked, shocked.

"Yes," Eric said.

"I wouldn't get in there for all the money in the world," the driver mumbled.

It didn't take long to drive downtown to the central police station. There, in the basement, they opened the doors of the paddy and Eric led Gus out. The officers moved back quickly. The one with the rifle stood with his finger on the trigger. They had closed the big street doors so, if Gus got loose, he'd still be penned in this underground concrete room. Eric held the chain close to Gus's neck and the bear looked about curiously, his nose wrinkling as he sucked in the strange scents. His stubby ears were erect to catch the hollow sounds of the room.

The big officer said, "Tie him to this concrete post. He won't break the chain, will he?"

"He won't try," Eric said. "But the chain will hold him."

The street doors were opened again. The group of policemen drew curiously nearer and Gus looked back at them.

An officer in shirt sleeves came in, followed by a young man with a pencil and pad. The officer said to Eric, "All right, boy. Suppose you tell me what goes on here."

"What do you want to know?"

"Quite a lot," the officer smiled faintly. "Who are you? What're you doing with this bear? Where'd you get him? What were you both doing out on Marine Drive?"

Eric told his story again, interrupted by pointed questions. The young man was taking notes.

When Eric finished, the officer shook his head, "Of all the crazy yarns."

"It's true," Eric insisted.

"It could be, Reilly," the young man said. "He does have the bear."

"Look at him," Reilly said. "He's just a kid."

"I'm inclined to believe him."

"That's because you haven't been down here twenty years, Mason."

"Then what do you think of it?"

"I've seen too many oddball things to think. Maybe this kid's running away for some other reason. Maybe this is a publicity stunt. Some nut trying to get notoriety for a circus. It wouldn't be the first time such a trick has been tried. You know of a better way to get free advertising?"

"You can check out the boy's story."

"The juvenile authorities will do that."

"What's going to happen to us?" Eric asked.

"That's for the juvenile authorities to decide," Reilly said. "There'll be a representative here in the morning. I should send the bear up to the zoo, but it's closed for the night." He scratched his head, looking at Gus. "We've had everything here from dogs and cats to chickens and skunks. I guess we can keep a bear for a few hours. You can sleep upstairs in the hospital for the night. There's an extra bed."

"I'd better stay with Gus," Eric said. "He knows me."

"Maybe I can find you a cot to sleep on," Reilly said and left.

The young man grinned and held out his hand, "Bob Mason," he said. "Tell me, Eric, you didn't cook up this yarn about Alaska, the circus, and coming here to meet a man to go back North?"

"I couldn't think up such a story," Eric said.

"I doubt anyone could," Mason smiled.

"Are you an officer?"

"Nope. Reporter. So the bear's name is Gus?"

"Yes, sir. Gloomy Gus."

"Where'd he get that name? How long have you had him and how were you two brought down here? I'd like a few more details than you gave Reilly."

Reilly returned with a collapsible canvas cot and a blanket. "You think this will do you for tonight?"

"Yes, sir," Eric said.

Mason helped set up the cot. Then they sat on the cot and the reporter said, "You were going to tell me about Gus and Alaska and why you came down to the south forty-eight."

Eric told Mason how he'd found Gus and about Tatouche and Ten-Day Watson. Gus flattened out on the floor, put his big head on forepaws, and went to sleep.

Finally Mason said, "I'm going to roust out a

photographer. Be back in a minute."

Mason returned grinning. "One mad man. I got him out of bed. He'll be here in a few minutes."

"You're going to put Gus and me in the paper?"

"It's a good human-interest piece. I'm going to play it up for all it's worth. This is a quiet night. We might get a good play. Now, you're sure this is all true?"

"Yes, sir."

"And all the two of you want is to get back home?"

"Yes."

The photographer came in grumbling. "Getting a man out of bed in the middle of the night just to take a picture of a bear. You think people never saw a bear before?" He discovered Gus. "Wh-what's that thing?"

"A bear," Mason said.

"Oh, no!'

"Then what's he look like to you?"

"No bear's that big!"

Mason grinned.

"Oh, gosh!" the photographer said, "what a monster!"

"You're absolutely right. Now, how about some pictures?"

The photographer took half a dozen of Gus lying down. Mason wanted some of Gus standing with Eric. "How do we get him up?" he asked.

"If I had something to feed him, he'd get up for it."

"What will he eat?" Mason asked.

"Most anything. Candy, a sandwich, an apple."

Mason disappeared and returned with several candy bars. Eric broke one in two, held half under Gus's nose, and said, "Get up if you want it." Gus heaved to his feet, took it from Eric, and stood smacking his lips. The photographer kept snapping pictures until Eric had fed Gus all the candy. Gus pushed at Eric's hands. Then deciding there was no more, he promptly lay down again.

Mason said, "Okay. Now you get some sleep while I pound out this story." The two men disappeared, the photographer saying excitedly, "Listen! I want to be in on the rest of this."

Eric lay down and pulled the blanket over him. He trailed a hand over the side of the cot where he could touch Gus's big head. Officers continued to come and go and to look at Gus. Prowl cars and the paddy wagons drove in and out of the basement. There were constant sounds of voices, the hurrying of feet. Eric wondered what would happen to them in the morning. The old doubts poured in. Would they both be sent back to Henry Marcel, or would it be just Gus? What would happen to him now that Ned Strong had no claim on him? One thing he feared most. They might never again see Tatouche and Ten-Day Watson.

A hand was shaking him and a voice was saying, "Hey, you going to sleep all day? Rise and shine, boy. It's ten o'clock. Things have been happening."

Eric sat up and rubbed his eyes. Gus was standing beside the cot swinging his head, looking about. Light spilled down the ramp into the basement.

Mason shoved a paper in his hands. His voice was excited. "Read this."

In the center of the first page, four columns wide, was a picture of Gus and himself with his arm around Gus's neck. Bold black letters above the picture said:

GLOOMY GUS COMES TO TOWN

Gloomy Gus, a giant Alaskan Kodiak bear, and his master, Eric, are on the first leg of a long hitchhike that they hope will take them home. Where is home? Tatouche, Alaska — two thousands miles away. Last night they slept in the basement of the city jail where Eric told us the most amazing story this reporter has ever heard...

The whole story was there, just as Eric had told it to Mason.

"Front page," Mason pointed out, "and a by-line. I have a hunch about this yarn. The city desk's been flooded with calls for two hours, and even here at the police station."

"What kinds of calls?" Eric asked.

"People want to give you and Gus a home. Some want to adopt you, or give you money to get home, buy food, clothes. They want to know if the story's true. Where can they see you? A couple offered to take you north with them. Others want to buy Gus. Some local organizations want you to appear so they can sell tickets. Anything you can think of somebody'll call in about. Why, this story's over half the state already. It's been picked up by the wire services. My boss said whatever you want, get it. I'm hanging tight to you till this thing's wrapped up."

"That's good for you, isn't it?" Eric asked.

"It better be. I've stuck my neck out a country mile."

"I don't understand."

"I went for that story last night. All I could see was what a good story it'd make and what it could do for me. I gave it the works. It turned out better than I thought. Now I'm worried. The city desk questioned the truth of your story just as Officer Reilly did. But I talked them into it. Since then I've talked with a number of older officers here in the station, and, Eric, not one of them buys your story. If this is a phony, a million readers will crucify me and this career of mine will be as dead as the dodo bird."

"But it's true," Eric insisted.

"I hope so. I called Fir Crest last night after I left you. They've got a dinky little weekly and I know the editor. I rousted him out of bed and gave him the story. He went to see Marcel. Charlie, that friend of yours, said Strong pulled out several days ago, just disappeared. It seems Marcel has had second thoughts. He wants nothing to do with you or Gloomy Gus. He's afraid the whole mess is apt to get into court, and his circus could get some adverse publicity."

"Then that proves it's true," Eric said.

"Not quite. If this is a trick Marcel has pulled to get publicity for his circus, naturally he'd deny everything."

"But it isn't."

"All right. I'm going along as if I had no doubts. I have to. I've burned my bridges. I'm committed. For the moment, at least, I'm riding high and so are you. A big paper can throw a lot of weight your way. Now, how about breakfast? Hungry?"

Eric nodded. "And so is Gus."

"What shall I order for him?"

Eric told him and Mason gave the order over the telephone in the press room. Then they went out and up the street to breakfast.

While they ate, Eric asked, "What's going to happen to us?"

"Well, you're a minor. You'll come under the jurisdiction of the juvenile court. Normally they'd find a guardian and home for you until you're eighteen. They'd put Gus in a zoo."

"But we want to go home. I can live with Ten-Day Watson."

"We're going to do all we can to help you. There'll be a man from juvenile court to take charge of you this morning. Then we'll see."

When they returned to the station, a knot of people were milling about on the sidewalk. An officer was barring the door and talking to them. "We can't have you barging through here interfering with our work. This is not an exhibition hall."

"We just want to see him. A look, that's all," one young fellow said.

Mason steered Eric swiftly past them and down the ramp into the basement. "See what I mean," Mason muttered. "That story hit 'em right here, where they live." He tapped his chest over the heart.

Gus had finished eating and was standing quietly. A group of people, most of them officers, were watching him. A man with a movie camera was walking around Gus taking pictures. Gus turned his big head following the man with little pig eyes.

Mason squeezed Eric's arm. "Oh, man," he breathed,

"we hit the jackpot. The dignified-looking gray-haired man in the blue suit is the mayor. The tall, skinny, bald-headed guy is Mr. Jackson of the juvenile division."

The cameraman turned and saw them. "Hey, Mason," he called, "that the kid? How about a picture of him with the bear for TV news? Mr. Mayor, would you stand on the other side for a picture?"

Eric was shoved forward. The mayor asked, "Is it safe if I stand on the other side of him?"

"Yes, sir," Eric said.

"If you could feed him something," the cameraman suggested, "it would look good. How about a piece of candy? Anybody got a piece of candy?"

"How about candy?" the mayor asked Eric. "Could I do it, son?"

Eric nodded. "Yes, sir. He likes candy."

A bar was shoved at the mayor. He handed it to Eric. "Show me how."

Eric tore off the wrapper, broke the bar in half, and held the piece in his palm. Gus lifted it deftly and chomped noisily. Eric handed the other half to the mayor. "Let it lie in your palm. You won't even feel his teeth."

"I hope not," the mayor muttered. "All right, you ready?" The mayor held the candy in his palm and Gus lifted it quickly while the camera whirred. "I didn't feel a thing," the mayor smiled nervously. He turned to the tall, thin Mr. Jackson. "My office is being swamped with calls on this story. That's why I'm here. People want to know what we're doing to help this boy get home. That means what are you going to do?"

Mr. Jackson glanced about. "Isn't there someplace more private where we can talk?"

"The press room," Mason suggested.

Eric found himself being propelled with the others down the hall into the press room.

Mr. Jackson said in precise, clipped words, "The boy is only about fifteen. Naturally he'll be a ward of the court until eighteen. A home and a guardian must be found for him. The bear should be sent to a zoo."

"That's three years," the mayor said. "Why should our taxpayers support this boy when his home's Alaska? Can't the juvenile authorities up there take care of him?"

"He needs a legal guardian and a home," Mr. Jackson pointed out. "We must make some effort to learn what his real name is, unless he knows."

"I don't know," Eric said.

"Let the Alaskan authorities do these things. It's their problem. This shouldn't be our responsibility."

"But he is our responsibility until we get in touch with the Alaskan authorities and they can find someone who will assume his legal guardianship," Jackson said stubbornly.

"How long will it take?"

Mr. Jackson considered, "A couple of weeks, maybe a month."

"A couple of weeks! A month!" A small, thin man had come unnoticed into the room. He adjusted thick glasses nervously and said, "Good morning, Gentlemen. I'm Philip Houseman, the Golden Nuggett Cruise Line. You can imagine my amazement when I opened the morning paper and saw that our Gloomy Gus and the boy were at the Portland jail, instead of in Tatouche, Alaska, as I'd thought. Someone should have notified me. This is serious, believe me. Very serious. Our first cruise ship will pull into Tatouche within ten days with more than two hundred and fifty tourists aboard. Every one of them expects to see the bear. It is imperative, Gentlemen, that we get this bear and the boy back there ahead of that ship."

Mason looked at Eric. He grinned broadly and made an O of thumb and finger.

The mayor turned to Jackson, "How can you speed this up?"

"It takes time. Just to send a letter and get an answer would take at least four or five days."

"Phone," Mason interrupted. "My paper will foot the bill."

"There's no juvenile office in Tatouche. We will have to get in touch with authorities in Anchorage. The Anchorage people will then contact someone in Tatouche who'd be willing to act as legal guardian," Mr. Jackson explained.

"Eric," Mason asked, "who in Tatouche can they talk to about taking you over?"

"Ten-Day Watson," Eric said promptly.

"As I remember, you said he lived out of town. Who could we call in town?"

"George Summers or Eddie Lang."

Mason pointed at the phone. "There you are, Mr. Jackson. Go at it and don't worry about the cost."

"This is very irregular," Mr. Jackson frowned. "There should be an exchange of letters and…"

"Make the arrangements by phone now," the mayor interrupted. "Exchange your letters whenever you like. But let's get this boy and the bear on their way. How many days did you say we had, Mr. Houseman? Ten?"

"That is correct," Mr. Houseman said.

The mayor smiled faintly. "I see you gentlemen are well on the way to getting this boy and his friend home. So I'll leave it in your hands and get back to my office. Mason, keep me informed. Let me know if there's more I can do."

Eric was amazed. He watched telephone conversations fly back and forth from Portland to Anchorage, from Anchorage to Tatouche and back to Portland again. He lost track of what was going on. But he did know that when George Summers finished talking with the people in Anchorage, he called the Portland police. Eric could hear him talking with Mr. Jackson. George Summers yelled excitedly over the phone, "Quit worrying about who'll be Eric's legal guardian. I will, Eddie Lang, Ten-Day Watson. Why, man, this whole town will adopt him if necessary. Just get him and Gus back here quick! We'll do the rest."

Then Mason was grinning at Eric and saying, "You're set, Eric. You're going home. How about that?"

Mr. Jackson was shaking his head, half frowning.

"Highly irregular, highly irregular."

Mason clapped him on the back and laughed, "But we did it, friend! We did it!"

"How are we going to get them back to Tatouche ahead of that cruise ship?" Mr. Houseman asked.

Mason scratched his chin thoughtfully. "Well, now," he mused, "the boss did say anything to help. Let's see if they'll foot the bill for room on a cargo plane going north."

Eric held his breath while Mason called the paper, gave them the full story, and asked about the cargo plane. When he hung up, he was grinning. "Eric," he said, "you and Gloomy Gus were both born under a lucky star. The Portland manager of the Alaska Barge Company phoned the city desk an hour ago and offered to take you and Gus back north free. They've got a cage that they used last year to transport a polar bear for the zoo. They'll send down a truck with the cage this afternoon to pick up you and Gus. You'll be trucked to Seattle where the barge is about to leave. You'll be put aboard and eight days later you'll be on the dock at Tatouche. What do you think of that, my fine feathered friend?"

Eric stared up into Mason's grinning face scarcely daring to believe his ears. He heard Mr. Houseman say in a pleased voice, "They'll beat the cruise ship into Tatouche by a day. That's good, very good."

Pleasure surged through him then in a great tide that stung his eyes and tightened his throat. "I've got to tell Gus," he managed. "I've got to." He ducked his head and ran.

It was the middle of the forenoon eight days later when the barge crossed the blue waters of Tatouche Bay and pulled up at the ore dock. It looked to Eric as if everyone in Tatouche had turned out to welcome them home. There were Eddie Lang and George Summers. Joe Lucky stood by the open doors of the bus. Mrs. Allen waved her apron and shouted words he couldn't hear. Ted Benjamin and Bob Duncan clasped hands above their heads and grinned broadly.

Beyond the people and across the dock Eric saw the

town's one street with its business district. He was surprised that it hadn't changed somehow.

The crowd moved back to give Gus room when they stepped onto the dock. Eddie Lang shook Eric's hand, beaming, "We're sure glad you and old Gus are here."

George Summers said, "Eric, the whole town's out to welcome you home."

"Yes." Eric looked for Ten-Day Watson's old felt hat and snow-white beard. He didn't see them. A stab of fear went through him. "Is Ten-Day Watson all right?"

"Fine as frog hair," Joe Lucky piped. "Come on, I'll take you and Gus up in style." He waved grandly at the open door of the bus.

Gus got his head through the door and stopped. "He can't get in," Eric said.

The crowd laughed, and Joe Lucky said, "I'm sorry, Eric."

Eric said, "We want to walk anyway, Joe."

Joe Lucky smiled, "Sure you do."

The crowd let them through. They came into the old gravel road and started hiking up it. The day was warm. The sun was high in a cloudless sky. The whole world had burst into a frenzy of growth. He could see the necklace of white-topped mountains stabbing the clear blue. The air had the fresh bite of the sea and of spring earth and a million growing things. Eric filled his lungs and let it out and filled them again. Something inside kept swelling and swelling.

Gus trotted beside him. This time he was not holding back but plodding straight ahead, big head down and swinging. They turned off the road and went up the trail. There were the cabin and Friday Creek, clear, sparkling, and swift. Kenai rushed at them, barking wildly, whipping his tail in a frenzy. He tore circles around them, grinning from ear to ear. Gus stopped, threw up his head, and he and the dog touched noses experimentally. Sitka stood in plain sight near the creek willows poised for flight. He stamped his feet, shook his horns, and snorted delicately.

Ten-Day Watson came from the cabin. He looked just as Eric knew he would. His snow-white beard and scraggly white hair peeked from beneath the battered old felt hat. His eyes seemed a more startling deep-water blue than ever.

Eric said, "I'm back, Ten-Day."

The old man nodded. "I'm glad, son."

Silence fell between them. Gus sniffed a grass clump. Kenai danced around him wanting to play. Watson said, "You look a mite taller, seems like. And old Gloomy Gus is about two hundred pounds heavier."

"I guess so," Eric said. "We've been gone about six months."

"Six months and ten days this morning."

"The whole town was out to meet us," Eric said. "Everybody."

"I thought about goin'. But you always came up here. We met right over there."

"I'm glad you didn't come," Eric said.

Gus pulled at the chain and Watson said, "Turn him loose. The vanguard of the salmon run has already started."

"You think he'll come back?"

"Of course. Just as soon as he catches a couple of salmon."

Eric unsnapped the chain. Gus stood there, swinging his head, delicate black nostrils sucking in all the wonderful smells he remembered. Then he lumbered out across the tundra heading straight for his distant spawning stream. The old man and the boy watched him go.

"I haven't done anything to get ready for the tourists," Watson said. "I figured you'd want to help."

"That's about all I've been thinking of," Eric said.

"Then we'd better get busy," Watson grinned. "We got a slew of work to do."

They spoke only once of Ned Strong and of the juvenile court conditions. They had set the sluice boxes and were lying on the bank resting when Watson said, "Talked with one of them juvenile people. I'll be your guardian if it's all right with you."

"It's what I want."

"Man said he didn't think they'd find out much about what happened to your pa after all these years. Might not even find the diggin's. The Kantishna's a big territory." The old man broke a stick, tossed the pieces into the creek and watched them float away. "You got to have a last name. Lawyer in Anchorage can help us out. How about Watson?"

Eric rolled over, and the deep-water blue of the old man and the gray eyes of the boy looked into each other. "I'd like that fine," Eric said.

"Me, too."

Next morning, when Joe Lucky came up the trail at the head of the first bus load of tourists, they were ready. The sluice boxes were set. The gold pans were lined up on the creek bank each with a shovel full of gravel. Kenai, Sitka and Gus were there.

Ten-Day Watson stood before the people, combed his fingers through his snow-white beard, and went into his spiel. "I'm Ten-Day Watson. The dog's Kenai; he's part wolf. The deer's name is Sitka 'cause he's a Sitka blacktail. There's Eric, and the bear is that old Gloomy Gus."

## ABOUT THE AUTHOR

Walt Morey's life has been as adverturesome as those of his characters. He has worked as a boxer, construction worker, mill worker, shipbuilder, theater manager, and deep-sea diver. Born in Hoquiam, Washington, Walt has worked and lived in the Northwest settings for his novels. His love of nature and the wild, the land and the people, and especially the world of children and imagination stand out in his books.

Although he learned to read at a late age, he quickly turned to writing — first for the pulp magazines, for which he wrote short stories, and later for children, who became his primary audience.

Walt's books have twice won the Dutton Junior Animal Book Award, and his first book for young people, *Gentle Ben*, received an ALA Notable Book award before being made into a movie and television series. His *Kävik the Wolf Dog* also won the 1970 Dorothy Canfield Fisher Award. Walt continues to write and to be honored for his contribution to American literature.

Walt Morey and Peggy, his wife, live near Portland, Oregon, on the banks of the Willamette River, where they enjoy the wildlife of the waterway and the seasons of their orchard and the surrounding land.

# COLOPHON

This book is a reissue, without changes, of the text originally published by E. P. Dutton & Co., Inc., of New York. In all other respects, this edition is original.

The cover design is by Judy Quinn of L.grafix in Portland, Oregon. The cover art is by Fredrika Spillman of Mulino, Oregon. And the overall design of the books in the Walt Morey Adventure Library was under the direction of Dennis and Linny Stovall of Blue Heron Publishing, Inc.

For this trade paperback edition the type has been completely reset in Palatino and Optima, digital typefaces by Adobe Systems Incorporated. The text was set electronically at 10/13 in Portland, Oregon by L.grafix on a Linotronic 300 Imagesetter and printed on acid free paper in the United States by Delta Lithograph Company.

# The Walt Morey Adventure Library
### from
## Blue Heron Publishing, Inc.

The Walt Morey Adventure Library stands for the finest in juvenile and young adult fiction. Every title meets the most rigorous standards of storytelling excellence. Readers of all ages will enjoy these timeless, emotionally charged tales of action and adventure by the author of *Gentle Ben*, as well as new books by Walt Morey and others. The following books by Mr. Morey are the first offerings in the WMAL:

*Gloomy Gus*
*Scrub Dog of Alaska*
*Runaway Stallion*
*Year of the Black Pony*
*Run Far, Run Fast*
*Home is the North*
*Deep Trouble*
*Angry Waters*

These titles are available at your favorite bookstore or directly from the publisher for $5.95 each, plus $1.50 s/h for the first book and $.50 for each additional book (US funds only, by check, MO, or VISA/MC). Discounts are available for purchases of the entire Library or large quantities of individual titles. To order any of these books, or for a current catalog and price schedule, write to:

Walt Morey Adventure Library
Blue Heron Publishing, Inc.
Route 3 Box 376
Hillsboro, Oregon 97124
503/621-3911

BLUE HERON
Publishing, Inc.